The great gearshift lever of the *Chester Alan Arthur* was moved from one setting to another until at last the Professor seized the ornate steering tiller in his firm grasp and, cracked and disreputable briar held clenched in his large teeth, said, "Having made the few required adjustments to the controls, we find ourselves sailing into the blue, *on our way to the moon!*"

And so, on the morning of May 23, 1884, Professor Theobald Uriah Thintwhistle, with his protégé Herkimer and manservant Jefferson Jackson Clay, embarked on man's greatest adventure!

Into The Aether

RICHARD A. LUPOFF

A DELL BOOK

Published by
Dell Publishing Co., Inc.
1 Dag Hammarskjold Plaza
New York, New York 10017

Dell ® TM 681510, Dell Publishing Co., Inc.

Printed in the United States of America

First printing—January 1974

CHAPTER 1
Buffalo Falls, Pennsylvania

'Twas a glorious morning in the month of May, and the quaint village of Buffalo Falls wore her springtime diadem of bluest blue with a dotting of pure white fleece as gay *primavera* clouds drifted and wove through the azure of heaven with each puff of the cheerful warming zephyrs that mark the fertile valleys of western Pennsylvania.

Lawns were growing in the lush green of springtime's resurrection, and the glinting sunlight caused sparkling dewdrops to give back emerald green effulgence to the eye of the appreciative observer. It was a Saturday morning, the twenty-third day of the month, and according to the calculations of the venerated Bishop Ussher, the earth was precisely 5,887 years and seven months of age. As such she bore her centuries with remarkable grace and attraction.

Round about the neatly painted white frame houses of Sycamore Street the tall elms and ashes, poplars and oaks cast rounded pools of cool green shadow midst the Pennsylvania sunlight that warmed and illumined the peaceful town. Brightly tinted birds, returned from their winter's sojourn to more southerly climes, gave happy song as they worked diligently, constructing the tiny nests of twig and earth in which their delicately toned eggs would soon be placed.

It was upon this scene of innocence and tranquility that there impinged this morning the cheerful tones of a whistling youth. Small children abandoned their hoops and their golliwogs, and the town's canine citizens interrupted their four-legged frolicking to observe the sight that proceeded down the center of Sycamore Street's hard-packed earth surface.

For the joyous tune that penetrated the morning stillness this day had as its source a lad done up in the latest and spiffiest of garments available at Jeshaw Callister's Dry Goods Emporium. An impressive tweed jacket, tortoise-shell buttoned at the breast and belted in the rear, covered a blue-striped camisole with ivory celluloid collar and cuffs.

A patriotically dotted bow tie emerged from the rounded celluloid collar. Beneath the edges of the jacket there depended corduroy knickers, canvas leggings and well buffed but sturdy brogans. The young man who sported these garments was possessed of a fine countenance, a strong chin, even teeth, and straight and steely, well disciplined hair.

Surmounting his admirable physiognomy a straw boater, broad-brimmed and silk-ribboned, was set squarely and, lest a vagrant breeze encourage truant tendencies upon the part of the gay *chapeau,* an elastic cord ran from its curved brim to the youth's tweed lapel.

Most remarkable of all, however, was the whistling lad's means of locomotion, for he proceeded down Sycamore Street, past Washington Avenue, Jefferson Avenue, Lincoln Park and Ulysses S. Grant Square with its Union Soldiers' Monument, bravely if somewhat precariously perched upon the tall front wheel of a mechanical velocipede. This it was, rather than the tune or the appearance of the youth, however admirable those may have been, which attracted the attention of the young children and canines of the neighborhood, for velocipedes were as yet a rare and much admired sight to the residents of Buffalo Falls at the time of our narration.

While this amazing sight passes before our admiring eyes, let us close our ears for a brief moment to the cheery tune the lad is whistling and eavesdrop instead upon the thoughts passing through that portion of his skull devoted to *intellection.*

This delight-filled day is certain evidence of our Maker's benevolent attitude toward mankind, the youth is thinking. *I but wonder what activity occupies my mentor this morning.*

Ah, it is a clean and pious thought which first crosses the cranium of the young chap. May we never detect there a less worthy! But what can be the meaning of his second inkling, that which reflects a question in the youngster's mind? Let us not detain ourselves too long in contemplation of this matter, for answers to many questions, most assuredly including this one, are undeniably to be found if we will but persist awhile longer.

For suddenly, as the lad's velocipede draws even with a dwelling marked by gingerbread decoration of unusual and unexpected design, his orbs espy a sight of such astonishing nature that the rapidly revolving wheel fetches up upon the edge of the neatly planked sidewalk and our young man is deposited, with alarming precipitance, upon that very planking, losing his purchase upon the seat of his velocipede, his natty straw boater flying from his well-parted hair and returning with an unusual sound from the end of its sturdy tether, and a portion of his anatomy which delicacy forbids us to name making violent contact with the sidewalk, to the momentary distress of the young man but, fortunately, without causing visible damage to the corduroy knickers which cover that part.

As the youth rose from the undignified position into which he had been precipitated by his unanticipated mishap, he could be heard to exclaim in a highly agitated voice most uncharacteristic of his more controlled usual tones, the following sentences: "My stars! Is that not a deep and dark excavation which I saw in the yard behind Professor Thintwhistle's abode? If my senses have not taken leave of their owner, a most remarkable and mystery-filled incident must needs have transpired here!

"And, most distressingly of all to my mental self-possession, what can have happened to the Professor himself!"

Thus giving audible voice to his mentation of wonderment and distress, the puzzled chap carefully raised his disarrayed velocipede and leaned it carefully against the white picket fence which surrounded the neat home of Professor Theobald Uriah Thintwhistle, upon having done which he unceremoniously let himself through the latched gate by leaning over it and undoing the latch, and proceeded to cross the grassy plot in order that he might investigate the astonishing *hole* which so disfigured the well-ordered and neatly clipped growth which surrounded the Professor's domicile.

The young man advanced to the precipice-like edge of the excavation and, head cocked to one side, body inclined forward to assure him of an improved line of vision, hands placed almost carelessly upon the knees of his corduroy knickers, he peered into the opening in the earth.

From the darkness beneath the grass there emerged

a surprising—and even alarming—sound, that of a
shovel working upon the very earth, scraping and clattering as it struck the occasional rock which dotted the
moist black loam of fertile western Pennsylvania,
where was located the town of Buffalo Falls.

"Ahoy below," called the lad, delighting momentarily in the occasioned use of a piece of nautical slang
dredged by him from the latest thriller to emerge from
the prolific pen of his literary ideal Mr. G. A. Henty, a
thick and thrilling tome titled *With Nelson at Trafal-
gar*, which volume the youth had flaunted beneath the
noses of his fellow students at the Buffalo Falls Normal School in gleeful evidence of the superiority of the
aforementioned Henty over his arch rival for paramount auctorial honors, the equally famed Mr. R. A.
Ballantyne.

His borrowed greeting eliciting no response from
the darkness below save a continued grating of metal
upon soil and stone, the young fellow called a loud
"Halloo!" into the pit, which cry was followed by an
almost total diminution of the sounds of labor from
the hole. Taking heart from the new silence and deter-
mining to pursue the thus-far one-sided conversation
which he had initiated, the lad inquired loudly, "What
is going on down there? Is it you in the hole, O my
guru?"

From the hole there emerged a response almost
without delay, in a voice indicative of great maturity,
breadth of learning, noble refinement and a well-
rounded personality. In tones well designed to pro-
duce a reaction of confidence and joy in the auditor
was heard the statement, "Yes, Herkimer, it is indeed I,
for I am able not only to recognize you by your tone
and idiosyncratic choice of rhetoric, but am able, from
my position here in this place of darkness, to cast up-

ward my gaze into the sunlit day above, and perceive there your intelligent and perceptive countenance."

Young Herkimer—for that was indeed the *nomen* by which the lad was known—clapped his hands in joy at the response which his *halloo* had produced, and, first carefully brushing the grass with his neatly manicured hands to assure himself that he had select-ed spots from which the morning's dew had already been drawn by the warming rays of old Sol, knelt upon the greensward beside the hole in the earth.

Leaning carefully forward so that his physiognomy protruded over the edge of the excavation, the lad ventured anew to put query to his admired instructor and preceptor. "What activity occupies you so unac-customedly beneath your lawn?" he asked.

"Await me for one moment, please," the Professor responded, for he, as the instructor in dramatic decla-mation and natural philosophy of the Buffalo Falls Nor-mal School, was well accustomed to providing infor-mation and moral guidance to the young persons whose presence in that institution was indicative of their youthful enthusiasm for increased knowledge of the world.

"I will raise myself momentarily from the Stygian excavation," the Professor continued to declaim, "for I have foresightedly brought with me into this opening in the earth a well-made stepladder of adequate eleva-tion to permit my re-emergence from this hole virtual-ly at will."

So saying, the Professor proceeded to climb the very stepladder to which he had made oral reference, and, as young Herkimer rose respectfully to a standing po-sition near enough the edge of the pit to observe the emergence while yet retaining between himself and the lip of the excavation a space sufficiently extensive to assure that he would not tumble unintentionally into the hole, Professor Thintwhistle rose majestically from the subterranean darkness, his countenance becoming visible portion by portion as he climbed the ladder step by step.

As young Herkimer gazed admiringly at his elder, the form emergent from the excavation was seen to be surmounted by a liberal thatch of curled and lengthy locks, shading from a virile black through the steely gray of advancing middle years and on into the whiteness that presaged the arrival of a respected and well-earned seniority. A high and noble brow lined by the cares and responsibilities of its possessor's numerous years gave way to a pair of bushy eyebrows beneath which two piercing and knowledgeable orbs peered through shell-rimmed *pince-nez*. A well-formed aquiline nose could be observed, and through a still dark beard well salted and peppered with lightening streaks there was seen a mouth firm and strong.

For his exertions beneath the surface of *terra firma* the Professor had placed a workingman's smock over his own correct clothing, and as he stepped upon the grassy covering of the earth the older man removed this outer garment revealing his properly starched wing collar, striped cravat, carbuncle stickpin and carnation boutonniere.

Facing the youthful Herkimer, Professor Thintwhistle addressed himself to the lad in terms marked by a careful mixture of solicitude, affection, and authority. "Here am I, young fellow," quoth the Professor. "What mission brings you to my abode here on Sycamore Street this Saturday morning, and what service or information can I provide for the easement of your presumed mind?"

Young Herkimer cast his own eyes downward in

confusion at the warmth and vigor in his host's welcome; yet, determined to press on undeterred by his own youthful shyness, the lad pursued his initial line of inquiry by putting to his elder the following question: "What were you doing in that deep and dark hole, my revered leader?"

Professor Theobald Uriah Thintwhistle, or "Old Tut" as that element of the Buffalo Falls Normal School student population known as the school *wiseacres* frequently referred to him when the Professor was not within earshot of their impolite badinage, made response to Herkimer's polite inquiry after but a moment's hesitation. The manner in which he responded was not unusually remarkable, as shall be seen when his brief speech is recorded below, but before examining the words of the Professor's reply, let it be noted that a disquieting thought had its birth in the well shaped and thoroughly stocked cranial dome of the Professor.

This bit of mental inquiry went unspoken, but had it been expressed in audible form, the listener would have heard Professor Thintwhistle ask himself, *How can I be rid of this pestiferous nitwit?*

Pestiferous nitwit indeed! Ours not to judge the natures of our protagonists; ours merely to observe and report upon their actions, while the reader, undoubtedly an individual of independent mind and well-developed intellect, will form evaluations of his own. Nonetheless, one expects no such thought to cross the mind of Professor Thintwhistle as did in fact have being within his cranial cavity. Let us pursue this matter further, but first let us take note of the words which he addressed aloud to his young questioner.

"In this excavation of my own making, lad, I have

been engaged in the pursuit of labors of a highly confidential nature."

Thus spoke Professor Thintwhistle, a suitable if not overly illuminating response to the question put by Herkimer. But how out of accord with Professor Thintwhistle's *thoughts*. For, were we able once more to listen in upon the mental processes of the graying *savant*, we should once again take note of his thought processes producing a message on the following order: *I must dispense with the presence of this young fool!*

How now! Perhaps all is not as it seems. One detects a note of unexpected and even unpleasant nature in the outwardly charming and charitable person of Professor Theobald Uriah Thintwhistle. It may be that the *wiseacres* of Buffalo Falls Normal School had stumbled all by accident upon a truth far greater than merely acronymizing their preceptor's names when they saw fit to dub the elderly figure "Old Tut."

Still, reaching into a pocket of his immaculate but bulging coat, the Professor withdrew a huge and blackened briar and clenched large and well-anchored teeth upon its bit. Its bowl all innocent of tobacco, yet the pipe was a familiar prop to the Professor's students and associates, its presence in the very classrooms of the Normal School exciting wide comment from less eccentric members of the faculty, yet grimly maintained by "Old Tut" as a perquisite of his seniority upon the staff and his unquestioned expertise in the fields of his chosen profession.

With a briskness of step that belied the lines of his countenance and the loss of pigment from his hirsute adornment, the Professor led his questioner in miniature procession to the rear veranda of the white frame building which housed not only his living quarters but his library for the studies of natural philosophy and dramatic declamation. The *savant* unhesitatingly crossed the wooden portico, passed the lengthy glider which rested upon it beneath a hanging green, and opened the door to the rear parlor of his domicile.

With hardly a glance over his elegantly clad shoulder in the direction of the faithfully following Herkimer, the Professor ejaculated, "Come into the house and I will explain, my lad!" Another brief stride brought the Professor into his house, whereupon he continued, in part to Herkimer and in part to himself, "I will ask Jefferson Jackson Clay to fetch us tea."

"Oh, boy!" he called to the aforementioned servant, and, when the latter failed to respond immediately, grumbled, "Where has that lazy blackamoor got himself to?"

Hardly had the two companions of the grassy yard entered the parlor and planted their feet upon its thin but tasteful carpeting when there appeared from the pantry the servant whose presence the Professor had but recently expressed his desire to assure. The houseman was of tall and well formed body, properly dressed in white jacket and black bow tie with dark trousers and a perpetual towel draped over his left forearm. A craggy brow and large, widely-spaced eyes marked his dusky face, while a kinky coating of wool protected his chocolate poll from the rays of the daily sun.

Shuffling forward and bowing almost imperceptibly to the master of the household, the darky said "Yowsah, Mist' Pufessah, Ah's hyah!"

A scowl of anger and impatience crossed the face of the Professor as he stared furiously at the dilatory Jefferson Jackson Clay, then pronouncing his words with clarity and care, the Professor shouted, "Fetch us some tea, you bloody baboon!" Without waiting for the colored man to disappear again into his pantry the Professor turned to Herkimer and explained benignly, "He is, of course, a simple child of nature. As all of his kind, he would be lost without us to provide guidance and discipline."

Ushering his young visitor to a wicker-work seat and ensconcing himself upon another of the sort, the learned Professor offered a smile of charitable interest and addressed himself once again to the youth. "Now, Herkimer," the Professor intoned sonorously, "if you will but enlighten me as regards the cause of your puzzlement and distress, I shall endeavor to relieve your obviously discommoded condition."

Young Herkimer breathed deeply, attempting earnestly to recall his lessons in dramatic declamation as received at the Buffalo Falls Normal School from the very man he now faced across the dust-free antimacassarred deal-top table, and uttered his inquiry: "Sir, as I was pedalling by upon my velocipede a mere few moments ago and chanced to note the excavatory process in your back yard, I was precipitately fired with curiosity as to the nature and purpose of the activity taking place."

The white-haired *savant*, taking but a scant moment or two in which to digest the nature of the youth's inquiry, rose majestically from his seat and, leaning forward as token of his earnest sincerity, addressed his inquisitor thusly: "My young friend, and, I may add, my student of dramatic declamation and natural philosophy whom I hold in high pedagogical regard, you have stumbled by merest happenstance upon a matter of such earth-shaking significance that I hesitate to provide you with full information; nonetheless, and the aforegoing notwithstanding, I would be loath to leave you intrigued, your innocent curiosity piqued but unsatisfied, and will therefore be willing to provide you with a thoroughgoing explanation, nay, better, a visual demonstration of the project in the interest of which I was engaged in, if you will pardon the levity at this moment, *lawner* excavation at the moment of your arrival at my abode this morning."

The Professor gestured dramatically in the direction of a conventional wooden doorway, saying as he did so, "Come with me, friend Herkimer, to the cellar of my domicile, and there I will willingly reveal to your dazzled sight my *astonishing invention!*" The last words were uttered in an intense whisper, the hearing of which sent waves of excitement tingling up and down the spine of young Herkimer.

The lad rose from his seat and without the ejaculation of a single syllable followed his mentor through the indicated doorway.

Wooden stairs debouched upon a large platform beyond and above which there towered a complex device which from the instant of his first seeing it both dazzled and impressed Herkimer as indeed the most marvelous and remarkable sight ever to befall his vision.

"This is the object of my subterranean efforts," the Professor intoned in explanation. "Behold you now the reason for which I exerted such effort in my private *anthracite mill,* wresting from Mother Nature's possessive grasp the fine anthracite coal in which our native region so famously abounds. The coal in turn, lad, will in due course serve as fuel for the boilers of the mechanical marvel of all the ages, none but Theobald Thintwhistle's incredible ether flyer the *Chester Alan Arthur,* so christened in honor of the Chief Magistrate of our great Republic, the unprecedented steam-propelled craft in which I and a carefully selected company of servitors shall amaze the world—the which you see now before you!"

Throwing wide his hands with astonishment Herkimer could but gasp in reply, "Hath Man dared too much?!"

CHAPTER 2
Revolutionary Hill

"Not so," rejoined Professor Thintwhistle, whose modernism and radical thought had often provided scandal for the whisperers and malicious gossips of the village and the Buffalo Falls Normal School, but who, possessing courage in full measure commensurate with his moral convictions, refused to yield a tittle in defense of his unconventional beliefs. "Had heaven not intended the *Arthur* to succeed, Pennsylvania were created void entirely of coal. Coal, coal, Herkimer, is the substance which I most require, and coal is the substance with which our noble State is most abundantly provided.

"Thus Nature proves her favorable attitude toward this high endeavor. 'Tis as simple as that, laddie-buck! There is that which I need, and Nature hath provided it. *Quod erat demonstrandum!*" So saying he clasped his calloused but clean hands behind his back and strode triumphantly about the observation platform, puffing the while upon his cracked and disreputable briar while Herkimer leaned across a cast-iron guard rail reaching in rapt fascination toward the well-wrought form of the *Chester Alan Arthur*.

The *Arthur* was indeed a glorious and impressive sight, her body constructed of wrought and riveted iron, observation portals here and there fitted with air-

tight insinglass coverings, huge vertical steam and
smoke vents rising in twinned formation from her
flanks, while giant covered paddle wheels featured either side. A small aerial screw with the familiar mut-
ton-chopped visage of President Arthur carved upon
its mahogany spinner was affixed at the nose of the
craft, while at her stern an auxiliary exhaust and propulsion device protruded. Other objects at whose nature and purpose, other than pure decoration, Herkimer could but guess, studded the *Arthur*'s skin. In all,
her length was several rods, a size larger in fact than
the cellar in which she was housed, while her volumet-
ric displacement would stagger the imagination of the
unwary inquisitor.

His dazzled innocence taking in the true magnitude
and beauty of the *Arthur,* Herkimer felt his attitude as
it were lifted from his very heart, altered and returned
to its place in that vital organ, so that the lad turned,
tears of remorse at his own unworthy reaction brim-
ming in his sensitive brown young eyes, and clasped his
hands in supplication while he sank humbly to one corduroy knickered knee and pled thusly of the mighty
inventor: "Is she fully manned, Sir? Have you room in
your crew for the faithless but chastened and repentant
Herkimer?"

Removing his cracked and disreputable cold briar
from his large and well formed teeth, the Professor advanced to stand beside the youth and placed his free
hand firmly upon the straw boater which Herkimer,
annoyed at its endless bobbing at the end of its elastic tether, had once more set firmly upon his pomaded
hair. "This day do I swear it, Herkimer, this twenty-
third of May, 1884, do I affirm by all that Man holds
Holy—I *shall* take you with me, and Jefferson as well,
and the three of us shall *astound the world!*"

At this dramatic and emotion-filled juncture there was heard a timid scratching at the door through which the two had previously passed, and as the portal opened a crack there proceeded through it a mewling calico mother and her brood of parti-colored kittens, frolicking and tumbling down the steps to the platform where stood the tableau of mentor and disciple, followed shortly by the shambling, lackadaisical presence of the darky houseboy, Jefferson Jackson Clay.

Stumbling comically down the stairway so as to come repeatedly within a hair's breadth of sending his burden clattering about his large and splay-toed feet, the blackamoor announced majestically, "Ah's brought yo' tea lak yo' sed, Pufessah!" Simultaneously there passed through the black man's head the following thought: . . . *and spiked it with a slow-acting addictive poison, Charlie!*

The Professor withdrew his hand from Herkimer's bonnet and whirled to face the newcomer while Herkimer rose to his feet in flustered surprise. "Put that tray down, Jefferson, and attend my words!" he roared in the tone customarily utilized in addressing the slow-witted and cowardly but withal loyal and amusing darky. "I have something to say that will stagger your childlike, undeveloped brain!

"Jefferson, I am taking young Master Herkimer with me, and your dusky self as well, and we are all the three of us *going to the Moon!*"

At these words from his employer the Negro fell to his knees, where those joints persisted nonetheless in striving manfully to knock together in terror. Beads of cold sweat broke out upon the servant's black brow, and in a voice pitiable with its terrified pleading Jefferson shrieked, "Lawsa Marcy! Don' yo' say that, Pufessah! Yaw'll frighten me white ef yo' talk 'bout things lak dat!"

"Little danger of that," replied the Professor with a hearty chuckle. Then, with the air of a busy man of authority turning from unaccustomed levity to the serious business of the hour, he returned to the harsher and more emphatic tones previously used with the servant, and, pointing his forefinger angrily at the trembling and cowering darky, Professor Thintwhistle announced "Nevertheless, you simpleton, you will do as you are told and live to praise the day I took you in. Prepare to depart at once!"

"Yowsa boss!" the quivering Negro managed to quote. "But what Ah s'posed to *do?*"

"Dolt!" exploded the Professor. "We are going on a lengthy excursion. Make for your pantry and begin at once the transfer of a suitable variety and volume of condiments and victuals from thence to the galley of the *Chester Alan Arthur!*"

As the darky disappeared once again the Professor turned to Herkimer and, a merry twinkle apparent in his elderly but still lucid orbs, drew from behind him two costumes of a sort vaguely familiar to the young lad, but yet of a distinctive styling such that Herkimer found himself straining at his wits' end in an unsuccessful effort to identify the purpose of the unusual garments.

One of them, which the Professor clutched closely to his own well formed and manly bosom, seemed to be a rubberized, one-piece covering, its shoulders surmounted by glistening epaulettes of golden threadwork and streamers; from one epaulette-laden shoulder there depended a *fourreguerre* of similar splendor, while a broad decorative sash engirdled the suit at its waist; a narrower but still generous sash of golden silk crossed the garment from shoulder to waistband, while rows of colorful orders spangled the breast and broad golden stripes surmounted by loops of similarly xanthically tinted material circled the cuffs.

The second garment, which the Professor extended toward Herkimer, appeared similar in design and construction to the first, save for its spartan lack of decor. Its dark blue rubberoid construction was plainly visible, however, while that of the first garment was barely available to the eye for having been covered by trim. Cadet-type shoulder boards were attached in place of epaulettes; a narrow pocketed belt substituted for the broad cummerbund; and a pair of modest chevrons were attached to the sleeves.

"You see, dear lad," chided the Professor as Herkimer cast his admiring glance at the two habiliments, "fortunately I have the pleasure to be the possessor of several oceanic diving uniforms, the attachment to which of appropriately fitted helmets, gloves and boots will provide for us protection in the thin atmosphere of our celestial companion, *la lune*."

Handing the plainer of the two outfits to Herkimer, who proceeded without delay to don the unusual garment so as to assure himself of the correctness of its fit, which, indeed, proved to be admirably correct and offering no discomfort or difficulty save as it required the removal of Herkimer's straw boater before the diving helmet could be placed over the lad's head and properly affixed to the collar of the suit itself, the Professor produced still a third diving costume from the trove which had already provided his own and Herkimer's unconventional travelling outfits.

The third diving suit was old and tattered, wholly devoid of ornament, yet its plain material was colored by the presence of numerous patches of odd and contrasting tones, the whole offering an appearance of genteel poverty, so as to provide a costume of serviceable but unluxurious nature as was befitting to the station of its intended wearer.

"This is far better than the Ishmaelite deserves," the Professor intoned splendidly, "for just think, laddie, that without us to guide him along the revealed pathways of righteousness and civilization, the black fellow would to this day be nothing more than a naked savage scratching in some pestilential forest for his very existence—while in the domestic service of us, his natural betters, he is adequately fed, clothed, kept clean and educated in the ways of rectitude and proper behavior.

"Come then, my young companion, let us load our exploratory garments aboard the *Arthur* and begin to prepare her for her overland journey to Revolutionary Hill from whence she shall be launched smartly upon her historic journey!"

So saying, the Professor shouted again for the black Jefferson to appear, and issued to him instructions, having care to make each command as clear and emphatic as it was humanly possible to make it, in order that the limited power of comprehension of the black man not be strained beyond its capacity. At length the Negro, having to outward appearances at least conquered his ignorant terror of that which lay ahead for the travelers, proceeded to his initial duty station, which was at the cellar door, which he opened to permit the momentary egress of the mighty craft.

Climbing down a metallic ladder from the side of the observation platform, Professor Thintwhistle gingerly made his way across the upper deck of the *Chester Alan Arthur* and, pausing first at two stanchions previously prepared for this purpose, affixed to each a brave silken emblem; upon the one a miniature of Old Glory, its forty-six stars on their field of blue and the stirring stripes of red and white bordered uniformly in a xanthic fringe reminiscent of that which decorated the Professor's space habiliment; the other, the brave puce and cerise pennant of Buffalo Falls Normal School. Having accomplished this task the Professor advanced further toward the bow of the *Chester Alan Arthur*, in the due course of time arriving at the forward observation portal of the control cabin of the brave craft. He paused to extract a ring of keys from his pocket, then bent, made open a hatch beside the observation portal, and climbed within.

Meanwhile young Herkimer had followed "Old Tut" down the ladder onto the hull of the *Arthur*, and, at the urging of the Professor, and with a fine chamois cloth provided by the latter, having previously seated himself astraddle the port exhaust funnel, proceeded assiduously to the cleaning and polishing of that device. As he worked cheerfully away at his task, which he had not selected spontaneously but which he had willingly acceded to perform at the urging of the Professor, the youth resumed that musical activity in the pursuit of which he was engaged when first we encountered him pedalling his tall velocipede down the center of Sycamore Street. So do our habits persist!

Herkimer scrubbed and polished, polished and buffed until the port exhaust shone like a Civil War cannon in Buffalo Falls' memorial square, upon which achievement Herkimer proceeded to transfer himself from the port to the starboard exhaust stack, noting in the midst of his precarious passage laterally across the hull of the *Chester Alan Arthur*, that the ship had jiggled several times, and seemed indeed to be moving across Professor Thintwhistle's cellar!

Yes, for while the Professor was setting out his banners and then checking his handiwork for perfection, and while Herkimer was diligently pursuing his newly-assigned duty as the ship's brass boy, at least *pro tem*, the woolly-pated Jefferson Jackson Clay was also pursuing his own instructions, applying to the accomplishment of his tasks all of the devoted and even passionate loyalty so often felt by members of the lesser orders of Mankind when they receive kind and just treatment at the hands of the more advanced.

Jefferson had carefully lifted the hull of the *Arthur* from its cradle and slipped beneath it a sort of chained giant Irish mail cart, a child's plaything which had achieved some popularity in the smaller towns of western Pennsylvania and a number of other localities. As soon as the *Arthur* was securely mounted upon the Irish mail, Jefferson unwound from about his waist a heavy chain of remarkable length and strength, and attached it to the front of the first section of the Irish mail upon which the *Arthur* stood at rest.

At a shouted command and a wave through the observation window, both of the aforesaid signalling devices specified and produced by the masterly "Old Tut," Jefferson put his shoulder into his task, struggling to drag the towering *Arthur*, Professor at the as yet unactivated controls, Herkimer merrily esconced upon the exhaust stack, polishing, whistling, and occasionally bursting in upon his own song with exclamations of various description, such as, *"Just to think of it. I, the lucky Herkimer, a member of the Professor's expedition! How the fellows shall pluck at my clothing in envy!"*

No sooner had the *Arthur* cleared the cellar doors of Professor Thintwhistle's house, Jefferson momentarily grounding his tow chain as if it were an anchor and racing to close the cellar doors behind the trio, than Professor Thintwhistle, thinking to encourage the sweating darky, cried again: "Off to Revolutionary Hill, Jefferson—we shall use its gentle incline to gain a burst of flashing speed in which to accomplish the launching of our lunar exploration vehicle!"

The serving-man again took up his burden and, with a, for him, spirited "Yowsah!" cast back over his shoulder, hauled mightily upon the chain attached to the Irish mail upon which rested the graceful bulk of the marvelous creation in which they were to traverse the blue sky and black limitless space of the celestial dome, at the same time, however, thinking *This could not possibly work out better for the accomplishment of my sinister plan!*

Thus stationed at the Professor's behest, Herkimer gladly working to impart a final sheen to the exterior accouterments of the *Chester Alan Arthur*, Jefferson Jackson Clay straining his every muscle to tow the brave craft through the quiet, tree-lined lanes of Buffalo Falls and the Professor himself giving the instruments of the flyer their final examination in the rococo comfort of the Kermanshah-carpeted and maple-paneled captain's quarters, the mighty vehicle proceeded toward Revolutionary Hill to the cheers of awe-stricken children and the barks of puzzled mongrels. At length, having reached the crest of the highest peak within the village-incorporation limits of Buffalo Falls, the *Arthur* ground to a halt. Jefferson unshouldered his chain, casting it as well as his own lazy hide to the ground in the shadow of the bow of flyer until Professor Thintwhistle, drawing the isinglass curtains of the captain's quarters, shouted at him to look lively and bring his worthless presence inside the ship, lest it roll across his black carcass when the propulsion lever was thrown. Trembling as he so often did, the darky clambered upright, moving as rapidly as ever he did, and climbed laboriously up the side of the *Arthur* to the servants' entrance, through which he made his ingress into the ship.

Herkimer also, noting that final preparations were being made for the departure of the *Arthur* from the crest of the hill, climbed back down from the exhaust stack, giving its brass trim a final swipe with his chamois as he turned to make his way through the Arthur's main hatch.

In a matter of moments the stalwart three were gathered in the captain's quarters. Professor Thintwhistle delivered to Herkimer and Jefferson, with brief explanatory asides to the latter in order that his simple brain might not be unduly taxed, an inspiring address which concerned itself with the historic and unprecedented nature of the voyage they were about to undertake, the perils with which they would in all likelihood be faced, the challenges which lay ahead, and the glorious role which they would fill in the history of the Commonwealth of Pennsylvania and the Republic should they return successfully from their expedition.

At the termination of the Professor's remarks Herkimer applauded loudly and Jefferson broke into a comical cakewalk of joy, for all as if he had understood every word that had been spoken. Soon the two had subsided, and Professor Thintwhistle turned to the more immediate requirements of the moment. Signalling for the attention of Herkimer and the African, he set several controls on the captain's panel, pulled the lever which controlled the *Arthur's* propulsive

mechanism, and, facing his two subordinates said,
"Now, fellows, follow me as I jump up and down to
give the *Arthur* her start."

He began to leap into the air, striking the Kermanshahan carpeting with his boots, leaping again, working his arms upward and downward to increase the im-
petus of his impact. Quickly Herkimer comprehended
the Professor's intention and began to duplicate his actions in careful synchronization with the Professor's
leaps and landings. After watching in obvious puzzlement for a time, Jefferson too began to imitate the
jumping of the Professor and Herkimer, and in a short
while the *Arthur* began to teeter back and forth to the
timing of the impacts of the three.

Higher with each rise and lower with each dip
moved the bow of the flyer, until with a scrape and a
thump she dipped over the edge of Revolutionary Hill
and paddle wheels revolving majestically, great clouds
of smoke belching from her exhausts, she tumbled
down the side of the hill, digging her carven bust of
President Arthur into the rich grassy loam of western
Pennsylvania, raising her tail into the bright May sunlight, turning end for end as she bounded and
thumped down the hillside.

As the *Arthur* moved more and more rapidly, Herkimer, clutching a stanchion for support, gasped admiringly, "We are moving, Professor! Your theories are
vindicated at last! Oh, how the scoffers shall blush in
shame!"

"Aye, lad," responded the bearded and bold leader
of the expedition, "didst doubt me ever?" Without waiting for a reply the Professor turned once more to the
controls of the *Arthur*. He turned a dial until an arrow,
festooned with cupids and curlicues, pointed to a certain mark whose significance was known only to "Old

Tut" himself. Switches were moved, some from up to down, some from down to up. The great gearshift lever of the *Chester Alan Arthur* was moved from one setting to another until at last the Professor seized the ornate steering tiller in his firm grasp and, cracked and disreputable briar held clenched in his large teeth, said, "Having made the few required adjustments to the controls, and placing in motion the gravitic bituminoid propulsors of the *Arthur,* we find ourselves sailing into the blue, on our way at last!"

Herkimer turned his gaze to the isinglass window of the cabin and beheld a sight which astounded his boyish mind. For the *Arthur* was in fact flying through the very air of Potawatamy County, Buffalo Falls already falling away into the distance behind the flyer. Revolutionary Hill resembled but a tiny mound, and the houses of the village which they had left so lately were but miniatures of themselves. "It is so," he cried, "and we are in fact rapidly approaching the Ohio state line itself!"

To the accompaniment of the *Arthur's* steam boilers pouring forth their regular and rhythmical *chufa-chufa-chufa* Professor Thintwhistle turned from his controls. He smiled gaily and to the servant said "Jefferson, some comestibles for Master Herkimer and myself with which to celebrate the successful commencement of our great voyage! You may take an extra tot of ginger beer in the servant's quarters."

CHAPTER 3
The Great Asteroid Mystery

Their initiatory celebration completed, the three dauntless travelers settled quickly into the routine of their new environment, accustoming themselves to the isolation of the interior of the *Chester Alan Arthur* as she sailed majestically, paddle wheels revolving, exhaust stacks smoking, beyond the uppermost reaches of the atmosphere of the planet from which their journey had commenced.

In the main saloon of the *Arthur*, while the servant Jefferson swept and dusted, whistling to himself all the while and jigging from time to time to the beat of those invisible jungle drums which every African carries with him deep in his blood at the joy of being permitted thus to remain in the presence of his betters, Professor Thintwhistle and young Herkimer were engaged in earnest discourse.

Herkimer, his tweed jacket and corduroy knickers spruce and proper, his patriotically patterned bowtie standing in bright contrast to a fresh celluloid collar from Jeshaw Callister's Dry Goods Emporium foresightfully carried at all times in the young fellow's pocket, addressed in the most respectful tones the following inquiry to his mentor: "Professor, despite paying close attention to your lectures in natural philosophy, I must confess myself unable to comprehend how the *Arthur* maintains her forward velocity here in the void of interplanetary space if, as you have intimated upon repeated occasions, there is in fact little or no atmosphere in this region; for, if the *Arthur* is propelled, as you have stated, primarily by the exhaust of expanding vapors expelled through the opening at the stern of our craft, how then is it that the *Arthur* is pushed forward through the void when there is nothing here to push *against?*"

Professor Thintwhistle, immaculately garbed now in a spiffy naval uniform of dark blue serge, brass buttons and golden trim, his peaked naval cap perched firmly upon his skull and his familiar cracked and discolored briar clenched firmly in his large teeth as he stood to the tiller of the *Arthur*, guiding through the maze of the universe that noble ship and the lives and destinies of her three courageous occupants, smiled grimly at the question which had been put to him by Herkimer and, locking the tiller and throttle of the flyer into the positions which they at the moment held, turned with forced geniality to the lad.

With one hand he withdrew the cold briar from between his large and even teeth, a sure sign, as those who well knew the Professor would be quick to testify, that he took the question with the utmost seriousness and would delve to provide to his inquisitor an answer both thoughtful and satisfactory. With the other hand he clasped the youth reassuringly upon one tweed-covered shoulder and, facing him manfully, asked a question of his own: "Why, laddie-boy, did your own pater never discuss such matters with you?"

While Herkimer digested this question and prepared to reply to it, the mind of Professor Thintwhistle was not idle. Indeed, the thought which fleetingly crossed the mighty mind of that learned *savant* was the following: *If he but knew what the ether-flyer pushes against, it might shatter the delicate equilibrium of his frail mentality!*

What the Professor meant by this remarkable, if unexpressed, sentiment we should greatly yearn to know; however, our fortune will permit no contemplation of the intriguing matter, for by now Herkimer had indeed digested the Professor's inquiry, and, having first removed from the breast pocket of his tweed jacket a bit of folded linen and dabbed a droplet of some sparkling fluid from a corner of his eye, cleared his throat to make ready his vocal apparatus and gave this answer: "He never did, O mentor, for my Old Dad disapproves of such modernities as are taught at the Buffalo Falls Normal School, and it is only through the medium of the intercession of my loving Mother that I am permitted at all to remain matriculated at that admirable institution."

Thus continued the conversation of the two, but while they were deeply engrossed in their pursuit of the understanding of the great and intricate universe in which we are all blessed to have our being, other events were transpiring in the immensity of the interplanetary void, events which in due course might have dire and far-reaching effects upon the three travelers in the *Chester Alan Arthur* and which, were we not presently to observe them, might later catch us off guard so as to leave us gasping and puzzled by their significance. Let us, therefore, turn our attention momentarily from the touching scene in the grand saloon of the *Chester Alan Arthur*, and turn our eyes elsewhere in the immense expanse of outer space.

When the Creator of the universe set His hand to its great work on the morning of October 23, 4004 B.C., He made not only the earth and the moon, the stars and the sky, as Man had once believed, but also several other planets not wholly unlike the earth. We know already of Mars, Venus, Mercury, Jupiter and Saturn; there are those among the astronomical fraternity who suspect that there may be yet others, too small, too faint, or too distant from our home to have as yet been discovered.

He created also those enigmatic smaller celestial bodies, the comets and the asteroids, tiny, planet-like objects which move through space in their appointed orbits as if they were the pitiful remnants of a mighty planet which existed at some ancient time, but which, whether through the intercession of natural disaster or the unwise application of unholy knowledge gathered by her human inhabitants, had long since ceased to exist as a noble spheroid, and had become, instead, a motley collection of oddly shaped and variously sized smaller bodies.

On just such a one, as it whizzed through the black void that fills the space between the worlds, there was now assembled a gathering of men and equipment that was likely the most oddly assorted and remarkable ever to be seen in one spot. A squad of Zouaves, dashingly uniformed and clad in maroon fezzes, equipped with the long-barreled and curving-stocked rifles of their Algerian homeland, stood arrayed with a motley gang of Zulus, the latter garbed in leopard skins and ostrich feathers, their shields of woven straw and their iron-tipped assagais at the ready. Beside them a unit of Tsarist cossacks, their tall felt hats cocked rakishly, their cartridge bandoliers crossed on their breasts and strung across their shoulders; a unit of Napoleonic guards in their red, white and blue dress, their blouses faced with silk and buttoned with gleaming brass; Roman legionaires, tunicked and hel-

meted beneath the *fasces* and eagles of their standards;
a gnarled and grumbling crew of cave men, nearly
naked and wielding wooden clubs and stone axes; and
Spanish conquistadores with their armor breastplates
gleaming. Crusaders and Chinamen, samurai and Incas,
Gurkhas and Maccabees, all were arrayed in full battle
dress and bearing their heaviest equipment of war.

Before them stood their commander, whom we shall
in due course meet. But first, let us return to the ether-
flyer *Chester Alan Arthur,* and reacquaint ourselves
with the condition and activities of her three inhabitants.

In the main saloon, Professor Thintwhistle and
young Herkimer stand beside an isinglass porthole
discussing the natural philosophy of space flight. If only
"Old Tut" would turn his attention from his young
friend. If only the lad would divert his eyes from the
face and gestures of his mentor for a moment, and
look through the isinglass to see the Doom Asteroid at
present so far distant but steadily, steadily nearing the
Arthur.

But they will not.

Let us listen for a moment to the present stage of
the conversation. The Professor is in the midst of a
peroration: " . . . and thus, my dear boichik, once the
ether-flyer is past the atmospheric blanket of our own
mother earth, and her paddle wheels, having lost their
purchase upon the gaseous envelope of that world,
cease to provide us with the vital motive force which
we require for the continued progress of our ship
through the void beyond . . ."

Yes, that is indeed the Professor.

And as for Herkimer, tears of joy and gratitude glistening in the corner of either eye, he gazes rapt at the
Professor, hanging as it were on every word, and ad-

ding only an occasional and nearly hypnotized mono-syllable: "Yes . . . yes . . . yes."

That is indeed Herkimer.

But while this census provides us with information on the present activities of the two occupants of the grand saloon, was there not a third occupant of the *Arthur?* Of course there is, and he is none other than the dusky Jefferson Jackson Clay, last seen ferrying a broom about the cabin while Professor Thintwhistle and Herkimer discussed the functions of natural phi-losophy. Jefferson is no longer in the saloon with his betters. Having completed the task of cleaning the floor of the saloon, he has returned his broom to its place in a small closet and retired, unobtrusively, to the servants' quarters. It is there that we find him now.

Jefferson, having solidly bolted the hatchway lead-ing to his quarters from the inside, had seated himself at a small table. From a place of concealment he had taken a helmet of unusual design, one equipped with rheostats and magnetos, wires and evacuated tubes, and had clamped it firmly to his fuzzy poll. A curling insulated wire led from the helmet to a panel of in-struments revealed with the unlocking of a roll-top desk which, when closed, gave no evidence of being other than an item of furniture discarded by quality folks and appropriated by one who might yet put it to constructive use.

As he worked sedulously over his instruments, Jef-ferson might have been heard by an interloper (save for their being none, the Professor being presently engaged in the lubrication of Herkimer's brain) to whisper softly to himself as he accomplished a se-quence of self-appointed tasks, "Hmm, ohmmeter re-quires precision recalibration. Rheostat control section completed. Carrier wave for compensation counter balancer in place! Polarity reversal field operation completion correlated! Wave oscillator performance as predicted . . ."

And then, as the valiant little craft bearing the three Buffalo Fallsians *chuffed* bravely through the emptiness of the outer expanses, the drawling and slovenly voice of the blackamoor, now trained to a totally unexpected crispness, crackled through the ether bearing a message of sinister and mysterious import, *"Agent Clay to asteroid army! Agent Clay to asteroid army! Do you read me? Over!"*

Reader! What can this mean? Is the hitherto apparently faithful J. J. Clay other than a dense but loyal African? And *who* are the polyglot troopers of the void?

In the saloon, all innocent of the treachery taking place behind bolted hatches, Professor Thintwhistle is approaching the climax of a lengthy but inspired peroration. "And so you see, lad, as long as our supply of pancake batter remains unexhausted, we need fear naught for having nothing against which to push!"

And Herkimer, his heart singing at the new wisdom and understanding but recently imparted by the Professor, throws wide his arms and cries out in his ecstasy, "O Jupiter of mind! O Augustine of soul!"

But in the servants' quarters, mysteriously garbed and grim of visage, the usually carefree blackamoor Clay is speaking into a carbon crystal microphone, and is saying, ". . . very well, I will see to it that we continue on our present course during your approach and landing. But hasten, 'ere the fools suspect that I am not what I appear to be, nor is all what it seems!"

Meanwhile, on the Doom Asteroid, there stood before the weirdly assorted army of Vikings and Villistas, storm troopers and centurions, a tall, slim figure in

British army khaki, tan garrison cap cocked rakishly to one side, sideburns long and curly, a monacle screwed into one eye, his jacket marked with the twin pips of a first leftenant of the Imperial service, field glasses and gas mask hanging about his scrawny neck, side-arm holstered at his Sam Browne belt, jodphurs tucked into puttees that in turn revealed glistening brown boots carefully cleaned by a cowering batman.

In his hand was a portable microphone, mate to that used on board the ether-flyer by Jefferson, and into it the leftenant spoke: "Yaas, fine, well, yaas, Blithering-Snipe here, old chap, and jolly good it is to be in contact again! We shall continue on our present course, reaching the *Chester Alan Arthur* at an estimated time of arrival of approximately 1500 hours, should be done in time for a spot of tea, donchaknow!

"And, oh, I say, Clay, I do wish your professorial friend had thought of some other name for that ship. I do admire your elegant president ever so much; it's a pity that his name will attach to a ship that's to be so hidjously blarsted from the heavens! Well, nothing we can do about that, I expect!"

And *still* in the grand saloon of the *Chester Alan Arthur* the Professor continued his tutoring of young Herkimer. " . . . and so you see, my dear ninny," he was orating, "*formaggio* will serve as well as *fettucini alfredo,* or buckwheats as waffles!"

"Oh fount of enlightenment," Herkimer commented, "O mentor sublime!"

While in the pantry Jefferson Jackson Clay was murmuring into his microphone sinisterly, "Listen, Blithering-Snipe old baby, I'm gonna split now and set the super-magnetic electronoidal attracto-generator in our engine room. Over and out!"

And on the Doom Planetoid, where First Leftenant

Blithering-Snipe had, perhaps significantly, exchanged his cloth cap for a flattened steel helmet, the reply was transmitted. "Very well, Clay old chap. We shall have to home in on your automatic signal. Keep the old magnets pulling, ha-ha. Here we go, and we'll see you soon on board. Ta-ta!" And meanwhile the dark thoughts crossed his mind: *And you, fool son of Ethiop, shall become smithereens along with your two friends! Old Leftenant B-S has a trick or two up his sleeve yet to be used!*

On board the *Arthur* Jefferson Jackson Clay turned off his mysterious equipment, removed the helmet that had been clamped to his woolly head, positioned it in its place of concealment, rolled down the top of the battered wooden desk at which he had been sitting, and fastened it securely shut in an unobtrusive manner.

Upon the Doom Asteroid, from which the *Arthur* could now be seen only as a tiny speck against the Stygian darkness of the void, Leftenant Blithering-Snipe too dismantled his communications mechanism and turned to address his oddly assorted army. "On your toes now, men! 'Tis a chance for death or glory which faces us this day! Let's be worthy of our marks!"

On board the *Arthur* Jefferson Jackson Clay quietly unbolted the hatchway leading to the servants' quarters and made his way, slinking in the shadows, to the power room. Here he set in motion a small but powerful device of sinister purpose.

Upon the Doom Asteroid, from which the *Arthur* could now be seen as an object as large as a man's torso in the darkness of the heavens, Leftenant Blithering-Snipe continued to address his men. "Yes, you soldiers of the Empire, it's a stiff upper lip today and a liberty in the native quarter tonight, for you swarthy chaps, and for the rest of us, a do at the Empire Cotillion!"

On board the *Arthur* Jefferson Jackson Clay valved extra water into the boiler that furnished the steam that kept the ether-flyer moving steadily through the void.

Upon the Doom Asteroid, from which the *Arthur* could now be seen as a craft of astonishing size, virtually filling the sky of the tiny planet as it blocked out the void beyond, Leftenant Blithering-Snipe turned from addressing his men and, looking skyward at the *Arthur* which filled his field of vision, exclaimed "Oh, I say there, she *is* a trifle larger than I'd anticipated!" And the steady *chuf-chuf-chuf* of the *Arthur* boomed from the sky of the Doom Planetoid virtually drowning out the words as they were spoken.

On board the *Arthur* Jefferson chuckled fiendishly!

On the Doom Asteroid Leftenant Blithering-Snipe watched the *Arthur* grow and grow; the asteroid was now only as large as her paddle-wheel, now only as large as her smoke-stack, now smaller even than the opening through which black smoke was pouring.

Chuf!

Chuf!

Chuf!

The sound filled the sky! Leftenant Blithering-Snipe cried out "Good Lord, men, she's a regular bloody leviathan she is! *Help! Stop! Jefferson!*"

But there was no response from the blackamoor, and the Doom Asteroid, in relation to the *Arthur* no larger than a potato, swept into the smokestack of the ether-flyer with a mighty *swoosh*, there to tumble upon the coals in the furnace of the craft.

As his men sizzled and crisped, frantically firing their tiny weapons in all directions, but to no ef-

fect, before expiring, Leftenant Blithering-Snipe
turned his face heavenward, where a square iron door
clanged open and a huge, wool-covered dusky face
glared down, grinning fiendishly. Blithering-Snipe
moaned a single, final word, a hopeless, despairing
"H-e-e-e-e-l-l-p!"

And the last words to smite the blistering ears of the
villainous officer before he passed to that final parade
ground in the sky was the deafening whisper, "The
fire *this* time, baby!"

CHAPTER 4
Land Ho!

Thus passed from this physical plane Her Majesty's Loyal and Industrious First Leftenant Oswald Henry Victor William Fitzbeowulf George Blithering-Snipe and all the ill-matched minions of his polyglot corps, whilst upon the *Chester Alan Arthur* life continued apace, the diurnal routine of shipboard duties marching uninterrupted by even the slightest suggestion of untoward activity on the part of the dubious bushman.

In the main saloon of the intrepid craft the Professor paced up and down, cracked and infamous briar clenched firmly in his large and evenly arranged molars, an occasional ashy particle rising vagrantly from the blackened bowl of the smoking instrument, which particle, should it happen to light upon the *savant's* immaculate costume, was summarily dispatched by a flick of his sturdily constructed but neatly manicured digits.

Waving arms akimbo, muscular lower limbs moving widdershins, graying locks streaming in the airy confines of the saloon, "Old Tut" held forth a continuing peroration of natural philosophy and dramatic declamation for the sole benefit of the worshipful and devoted lad Herkimer, who stood, an expression of rapt dedication upon his youthful and unspoiled "phiz," Callister's Choice brand straw skimmer firmly set upon his own neatly-trimmed hirsute adornment, gratefully drinking in the wisdom being showered down upon his spongelike intellect by the ever-flowing fountain of beneficent wisdom with whom he had the unbounded fortune to share that Kermanshahán-carpeted compartment.

"The learned Philmus himself states that 'Commonsensical notions of what constitutes reality do not seem to apply to the fantastic state of affairs,' " the Professor declaimed dramatically, " 'the scientific rationale, in other words, does not simply mediate between fantasy and reality; it may also indicate a satiric correspondence between the two.' "

"Ibid!" exclaimed Herkimer, striking himself violently upon the peak of his cranium (all unmindful of the presence of his skimmer) as if to aid himself in understanding the Professor's pointed citation. "Oh, ibid!" repeated the sterling youth, "op cit, and kewvee as well!"

"Ay, sonny-child," exploded the *savant*, affectionately clapping the lad upon his tweed-clad back, "you seem at last to be coming to grips with the deformation and displacement of reality set forth in the crystalline verbiage of the learned Philmus, a man but little less wise and wit-filled than old Thaddeus Unganno Thintwhistle, mine own Old Dad, long though has he been gone to his reward in that great Normal School in the sky."

For the barest fragment of a moment there might have appeared, trembling and glistening by the warm gaslights of the *Chester Alan Arthur*'s wood-paneled saloon, a droplet of moisture in the grizzled old eye of the grizzled old pedagogue, but as happens so often upon this, our own earthly plane, yet even there in that perilous shell hurtling at a mad speed of scores of

miles to the hour through the thinly populated regions
of the outer ether, an interruption occurred which prevented "Old Tut" from yielding to that momentary
weakness brought upon him by the mention of the
cognomen of his own dear Old Dad.

"Ah's brought yo' yo' drink, Pufessah, sah, an' one
fo' de young gennulman."

'Twas the villainous Clay! Shuffling lazily into the
saloon from his pantry, the blackguard of a darky had
utterly doffed his weird and futuristic garb, and stood
transformed into his more accustomed self, collared
and liveried with a pristine towel draped across one
white-sleeved arm and balanced precariously upon a
horny palm a serving tray.

Upon the tray stood two heavy schooners of foam-
surmounted comestibles, the color of the liquid contents disguised by the verdant bodies of the fluted vessels, the snowy bubbles of froth streaming over the
edges of the containers to vanish mysteriously before
reaching the tray upon which stood the thick-walled
mugs.

We have unfortunately insufficient time to devolve
upon the little-known scientific marvel thus demonstrated by the unconventional conduct of the foam in
the cabin of the ether-borne craft, but diligent application to the study of natural philosophy will no doubt
quickly familiarize the reader with the principle in-
volved, and experiments in the homes and stables of
the nation's youth will serve not only to verify this
mystifying wonder of nature, but to encourage the development of a sturdy and inquiring nature on the
part of the very lads to derive entertainment as well as
enlightenment thereby.

On, though, with our tale!

The sturdily constructed Professor, sharp ears perceiving the slovenly and unpolished announcement of the blackamoor, sought pardon of his youthful compatriot to interrupt his own lecture, and, carefully removing his cracked and garrulous briar from its firm place between his sizeable bicuspids whirled upon the Stygian-complected servitor and exclaimed, "You dusky rascal! Where have you been?"

Not pausing for the inevitably slow and unsatisfactory reply which must needs issue in dilatory fashion from the broad and flabby lips of the African, Professor Thintwhistle continued as in an aside, "Oh, why ever did civilized, Christian, English-speaking man ever deceive himself as to the educability of the lesser races?"

E'en young Herkimer, the lad who had stood unspeaking throughout the arrival of the blackfellow and the Professor's ensuing comments, saw fit to interject a diffident comment of his own, to wit, "Ninny."

Well-justified ire curling up the flesh of his clean and line-marked countenance, Professor Thintwhistle pointed an angry digit to the deal-topped table which stood in the center of the saloon, and in his kindly manner barked an instruction to the black man. "Just put it on the table and get out of here, you inept buffoon!" he shouted.

The darky carefully lowered his tray to the antimacassar which covered the polished mahogany tabletop, revealing thus to the viewer's eye the presence beside the two schooners of a small number of golden-hued and sodium-chloride-flecked edibles, each bent through a curious series of convolutions so as to form a combination of curves and lines that dazzled the mind of Herkimer.

The African could not hold himself from responding verbally to the statements of the Professor, and so, giving vent to that inevitable feeling which fills any human breast upon receipt of a tongue-lashing, however mild and well-deserved it may be, the servant let fall from his pendulous lips a servile "Yowsah!"

The while there passed through his simple and undeveloped brain thoughts of a different nature. Again, let us invade the woolly pate of the simple serving man and examine the thought which occupies his primitive mind. It is: *Go on, fools! Lord it up while you can! That militaristic imperialistic fascist colonialist lackey Blithering-Snipe and his decadent clique of exploitative running dogs have got theirs! Soon I'll see to it that you get yours, too!*

What ingratitude is this?

What strange and perverse sense of disloyalty sends the blackamoor's simple intellect down such a path as this? What treachery does he plan? Will the *Chester Alan Arthur* ever reach the moon? And if she does, what manner of world will they discover? Can the noble Professor Thintwhistle and his sincere acolyte, the well-meaning, if not overly bright, Herkimer detect and overcome the mischief to be worked by the ungrateful and arrogant black Jefferson Jackson Clay, or will he succeed in sabotaging their grand adventure?

Let us skip forward in time, passing without pause over days of shipboard routine, of careful management of the *Arthur* by her onlie begettor and captain, the Professor; of the performance by Jefferson of those simple and repetitious duties to which his untutored brain is suited; of the many hours spent by Herkimer honing the edge of his fine mind and filling it with gems filched from the willing Professor T.

Let us instead drop in, as it were, on the courageous ship *Chester Alan Arthur* as she makes her way, boilers *chuffing*, paddle wheels revolving through the universal ether, away and away from the kindly environs of Mother Earth.

Upon the Captain's Veranda we find Theobald Uriah Thintwhistle sedulously examining a variety of indicators and controls, running a blunt and work-hardened finger from button to knob, from knob to dial, from dial to switch, and from switch back to button. A worried expression is apparent on his care-lined but courageous countenance. He thinks: *I'm sure this one does something. If only I could remember what!*

At the rear of the Captain's Veranda, where a short flight of stairs connects the Spartan and instrument-cluttered work area with the more luxurious quarters of the saloon, can be seen Jefferson Jackson Clay, hefting a broom in his customary lackadaisical manner. From his lips there rises a simple African song, syncopated in the natural rhythm with which a just Nature compensates the lesser races for their lack of more refined intellectual talent. "Eat dat chicken, eat dat chicken pie, oh my!" the darky croons to himself.

While inside his thick-skulled and curl-coated cranial cavity there transpires other business indeed. *Y'gonna burn! Y'gonna burn!* mentates the unreliable blackamoor.

And, esconced comfortably upon a tufted velvet divan of dark maroon shade, sits the innocent Herkimer, his eyes utterly imprisoned and his mind totally concentrated upon the risqué pages of a tattered copy of *Captain Billy's Whiz-Bang* which the lad had smuggled aboard the *Arthur* in an inner pocket of his tweed coat.

An observer present in the saloon of the *Arthur* would have seen tiny beads of perspiration edging

downward from beneath the gold-stamped leatherette
inner band of the lad's straw skimmer, might have beheld his eyes, round and protruberant, the palms of his
hands clammy with moisture. What sinister force
causes such alterations in the physiology of this traveler of the void? What influence causes the marked increase in his rate of respiration?

Is it Captain Billy's Pasture Pot-Pourri department,
featuring such thought-provokers and thigh-slappers
as the Aphorism of an Addict, "Dope deferred maketh
the heart sick?" Is it Captain Billy's witty philosophy,
as expressed in such dazzling one-liners as "The laziest
man I ever heard of was the one who said 'Whoa-back,
get-up' when currying off a mule?"

Ah, good friend, 'tis naught such! Beneath the eager
and innocent orbs of young Herkimer there are passing the *rotogravure* pages of the little journal, where
after an innocent enough daguerreotype of Captain
Billy's man Olaf feeding a cat her lunch, there follow
portraits of various ladies in thoroughly immodest
states of disrobement! Blame not the innocent boy,
blame instead the exploiters of youthful innocence for
publishing pictures with such aptly applied titles as "A
Brace of Heart-Breakers," or "Why the Scarecrow Ran
Away from the Farm!"

Ah, and credit the moral instruction received by
young Herkimer in his Potawatamy County home, and
the upright guidance of Professor Thintwhistle and
the staff of the Buffalo Falls Normal School, for the
lad's magnificent exercise of will. He raises tempted
eyes from the scandalous display of limbs and
shoulders! He flings his steely gaze through isinglass-
curtained porthole! The mental fantasy induced by
the illicit Explosion of Pedigreed Bunk disappears

with the *pop!* of a bursting soap bubble, and Herkimer beholds once more the splendor and the majesty of the void!

Stars crash, comets whoosh by the windows of the *Chester A. Arthur*, the very music of the spheres can be heard in the mind's own ear, while midst the distant clouds and shoals of the ether Herkimer beholds mayhap only in the eye of the mind—a diamond-bedecked image of the belle of Buffalo Falls' younger set, the luscious Lucille von der Lucans, daughter of the town's prosperous feed and harness merchant, old Heinrich von der Lucans.

But now, shimmering magically midst the starry spectacle of heaven's infinite dome, there swims into the view of the intrepid boy a silvery globe, her mountains and seas, plains and valleys delineated in the pale effulgence of old Sol's reflection, that glorious queen of the nocturnal dome whose nightly glow has inspired poets, philosophers and lovers alike from time immemorial.

It is—Ah, perhaps the astute reader will have leapt ahead of our narration on wingéd slippers of thought! If you have done so, perhaps you will bear with us as we inform the more slow-witted among the lectors of our inditement precisely what Herkimer cried out upon realizing the meaning of that which he now beheld, "Professor! Professor! I believe we are approaching a celestial body! What can it be?"

And Herkimer's mentor, raising eyes from the mystifying arcana of his own creation to cast his rheumy gaze through the very isinglass simultaneously penetrated by the glances of the lad, responded in tones of affectionate condescension, "Yes, Herkimer dear. For once in your idiotic life, you are in the *right*.

"My boy, the object which we now behold swimming gracefully in the blackness of the celestial ether is none other than dear Mother Earth's menstrual companion, that cold orb sacred to Diana the Huntress. 'Tis none other than the *Moon!*"

Upon the impingement of this startling intelligence upon the sounding drums of his ears, the lad, overcome with joyous emotion, flung his Callister's Best brand skimmer across the cabin and gave vent to a whoop of boyish exuberance, calling in a shrill and cracking voice, "Huzzah!"

Herkimer's skimmer landed upon the luxuriant Kermanshahan carpet near the place where the blackamoor cabin boy Jefferson Jackson Clay was pursuing his duties perfunctorily with the ship's broom. Upon noticing the arrival of the straw chapeau and hearing Herkimer's loud and enthusiastic "Huzzah!" the darky roused himself from his accustomed lethargic state and bent to retrieve the fallen hat. As he did so he clumsily dropped his broom and, in a state of simple-minded befuddlement at this new turn of events bumped his head with a resounding thump upon the lower edge of a small auxiliary control panel as he rose unsteadily to his normal bandy-legged stance.

The wise Professor and the eager-minded youth (we refer, by the by, to "Old Tut" and "Herk") laughed heartily at the simple fellow's state of mental disarray, and were chuckling still as Jefferson approached them, Herkimer's skimmer respectfully extended, mumbling incoherently all the while.

"Ahah!" the Professor exclaimed. "As well that you attend, Jefferson, for your services will be required as we commence the tremendously intricate maneuver of landing upon the surface of our earth's sister planet, for yes, the moon is no less a world than is the earth, for all that its size is less and its atmosphere attenuated."

(Author's note: The reader would do well to attend closely Professor Thintwhistle's peroration. It is scientifically accurate, having been checked and approved by the Publisher's standing Committee on Scientific Authenticity.)

"Now, Herkimer and Jefferson," the aged *savant* continued, "you must hasten quickly to the rear of the craft!"

Upon receipt of these instructions the two junior members of the *Arthur*'s crew precipitated themselves to the sternmost end of the well-appointed saloon, where the servant respectfully opened the hatchway giving onto the pantry, following the mincing steps of his social better through the neatly caparisoned servant's quarters, and through yet another portal to the chilly rear storage compartment of the craft.

As they stood there, awaiting further instructions, there rose an annoyed "meow" from the ship's feline matron, an outcry of protest from the cat mother at this, in her opinion, unwarranted invasion of the privacy of her "private" cabin. Echoing her loud "meow" were a number of smaller and weaker feline statements, the outcries of her brood of darling fuzzy kittens.

The while, Professor Thintwhistle had repaired once again to his especial kingdom, the Captain's Veranda, and, setting steely eye upon his target, the moon, and clenching his cracked and battered briar twixt large and firmly-anchored incisors, he tromped with one heavily booted foot upon the clutch pedal, shifted the position of the *Arthur*'s gear lever, spun the steering wheel earnestly, adjusted a captain's peaked

cap upon his graying locks, and called to his two helpers in the rear of the craft, "Excellent! We have
achieved the necessary eighteen-degree drift!"

He watched the surface of the silvery orb beneath
the bow of the *Arthur* as it turned slowly, craters, seas
and mountains passing in stately order such that, at
the appropriate moment, the Professor called again,
"Herkimer! Yo, you Jefferson! Now station yourselves
to starboard amidships!"

The two younger argonauts of space proceeded to
do as instructed, the blackamoor surreptitiously hanging back the tiniest bit that he might observe the actions of his white companion and ape them, the two
thus trotting rapidly back through servant's quarters
and pantry to station themselves on one side of the saloon neath an engraved portrait of the Professor's old
friend Zaghlul Pasha.

The *Chester A. Arthur* now swung behind the edge
of the moon, as she did so her entire intrepid crew
waving their caps—or, in the case of Jefferson Clay, a
clean towel—and giving voice to the brief but heart-
felt cheer of farewell.

This bit of business accomplished, the Professor
proclaimed "Back to work now, fellows! One each of
you to port and starboard, and then stand by for my
orders."

Herkimer started for the cozy book-lined nook opposite their present position; the simple darky Jefferson began to follow him only to tumble to the floor as
his big splay foot encountered the serene mother cat
who chose this moment to lead a parade of her offspring from the storage compartment into the saloon.
The confused servitor attempted to apologize to the
particolored feline, exclaiming, "Wha, Cleopatterah,
ah does beg yo' pahdon," to which the furry beast re-

sponded by pointedly ignoring the blackfellow and equally pointedly stopping to clean her trim and well-cared-for pelt.

"Ho, ho, you clumsy fellow," ejaculated Herkimer. "As well that little Cleo and her babies stopped you from tailing me, as you clearly failed to comprehend the Professor's meaning."

Jefferson remained seated upon the Kermanshahan carpet, absently tracing an astrological pattern in its oriental weave with one horny finger while Cleopatra called roll and inspected her tiny offspring for damage.

"Back to your place, Jefferson," called Professor Thintwhistle, merry eyes twinkling at the buffoonery of the cabin boy. "Now in concert, Herkimer and Jefferson, you must run back and forth, full tilt, swapping places with one another. Thus we stabilize our craft against the madly whirling ether currents set up by the natural defensive forces of the celestial moon."

As the two crewmen obeyed his command, dashing madly from starboard to port and from port to starboard, mimicking vaudeville routines, roundball hand-offs and similarly complex maneuvers with each passing in the center of the Kermanshahan rug, Professor Thintwhistle kept his keen gaze firmly fixed upon the lunar surface, ticking off landmarks as they passed beneath the mahogany hull of the *Chester A. Arthur*: the Mare Tranquilitatus, the Plaine des Jugs, the Lesser Himalaya Mountains, the Crater of Judges.

"Oho!" proclaimed the Professor at length. "I think I have espied a suitable landing place for us. Time, then, for you two lads to cease your activities and come forward to the Captain's Veranda! Herkimer, bring along Cleopatra! 'Tis but fitting that she as well

as the humans in our party witness this historic
moment!"

As the two ether sailors set reverent foot to the hitherto sacred territory of the Captain's Veranda, Herkimer holding the aloof Cleopatra in his arms and
Jefferson playing appealingly with the tiny kittens, the
captain of that lunar argosy pointed through his scrol-
lery-framed port to the surface below.

There, midst towering peaks and craters lay a lush
valley filled with greenery, tall trees reaching heavenward, rock-whitened brooks and lovely meadows filling the isinglass pane. "When we first set foot upon
the lunar surface I shall apply an apt nomen to this
new Eden which spreads itself so welcomingly beneath our craft," the Professor declaimed.

"Do you think the region is inhabited?" asked Herkimer.

"Lawsa marcy!" Jefferson blubbered, threatening to
break down in an access of gratitude and joy at the
sight of a homelike view from the ether craft. It is
doubtful that his simple brain comprehended the fact
that they stood a scant few miles above the surface of
the moon, and had not merely circled above the western Pennsylvania countryside and returned to their
original point of departure.

"Here we go now, lads," said the Professor. "As an
aside, Herkimer, the question of lunar humanity is one
which must needs await our exploration ere it can be
answered. Patience, lad, I understand!"

Shifting once more into low gear, the Professor
daringly double-clutched the ether-flyer's gear train
and left her steam engines idling in neutral. With the
gentlest of *chuf-chuf-chufs*, the *Chester Alan Arthur*
began to settle toward the ground.

The Professor wrenched his cracked and punctilious briar from between his teeth and began the count-down:

"Ecks!" he proclaimed.

"Eye ecks!"

"Vee eye eye eye!"

"Vee eye eye!"

"Vee eye!"

"Vee!"

"Eye vee!"

"Eye eye eye!"

"Eye eye!"

"Eye!"

There was a further pause, and then with a solid thud and a satisfying crunch, the *Arthur* rested upon the surface of the moon. The three ethereal argonauts congratulated one another, Cleopatra adding her own loud "Meow!" to the glory of the moment, and then the brave captain and crew commenced preparations to debark.

CHAPTER 5
An Unprecedented Predicament

The saloon of the *Chester Alan Arthur* was hushed as
the full meaning of this historic moment impinged
upon the consciousness of the three lunar argonauts,
each of whom, Professor Thintwhistle, young Herkimer, and Jefferson, paused to ponder, as well as he
might, the perilous journey just completed and the
wondrous adventures which must needs lie ahead of
them.

Let us once more eavesdrop.

Within the gray-haired cranium of Theobald Uriah
Thintwhistle, there passed in lightning-like progres-
sion, images of himself in his earlier years being hoot-
ed off the platform of learned scientific societies at
the proclamation of his theories of ethereal flight, of
his humiliated vow to prove to the world of natural
philosophy the validity of his theories, of long years of
secret labor in the cellar of his ancestral manse, of the
moral support received from Thaddeus Unganno
Thintwhistle, of the perilous journey and its triumphant outcome. *And as for this boob Herkimer,* he
concluded to himself, *I can see that extreme steps will
be required.*

And speaking of Herkimer, what pictures flashed
upon the magic-lantern screen of his boyish brain? His
own struggles at home, unkind teasings in the corri-

dors and parlors of the Buffalo Falls Normal School, his own good fortune in being included in the company of the *Arthur*, and the happy moment ahead when he could tell his Mom of his wondrous adventure on the moon!

Jefferson Jackson Clay stood with dull eye and nodding head, his expression vacant and his muscles lax. *Now we're getting somewhere*, he thought, *now if I can just make the right contacts . . .*

"Well, lads, let's to it!" the Professor's hearty tone broke the silence of the ether flyer's saloon. "As I have instructed you already, the atmosphere of *la lune* is a thin and frigid one, and were we to set foot upon her surface wearing merely our accustomed street dress, we should quickly come to regret our foolhardiness.

"Let us, then, bundle into our very warmest and woolliest coverings, lest we suffer extreme discomfort in the moments of lunar exploration, and return to Pennsylvania with sniffles to show for our trip!" So saying he strode purposefully to the chiffonier in which was stored his spare clothing, and drew forth a thick sweater which he pulled over his captain's jacket. This in turn was covered by a thick Mackinaw coat. His outfit was topped by a tall stovepipe hat and bottomed with a pair of wool-lined boots.

Herkimer and Jefferson attired themselves similarly, Herkimer however removing his straw skimmer long enough to affix a pair of warm ear muffs across the top of his pomaded skull and Jefferson turning down the flaps of a flannel cap to accomplish the same end.

Seeing to it that Cleopatra and her brood of tiny ones were supplied with ample bowls of milk and fish carried aloft for that very purpose, the Professor led the way to the main exit of the *Arthur*, permitting Jefferson to use this rather than the accustomed servants' doorway in honor of the historic moment. The Professor reached into a cupboard beside the door and removed therefrom a canvas-covered object some eight feet in length, which he placed under his arm before unlatching the chain which had held the door securely shut during their journey.

Professor Thintwhistle drew back the latch-chain, twirled a locking-wheel and cracked the *Arthur's* main door. There was a slight whoosh as the air within the cabin rushed through the opening, equalizing the pressure within the sturdy little ship with that of the frigid lunar surface.

As the door swung open the three gallant travelers peered around the corner; their six eyes beheld the first sight of lunar landscape ever to be viewed by earthly eyes from this close distance. The *Chester Alan Arthur* had come to rest, her paddle wheels unmoving and her mighty coal-powered steam engines at last turned off. The craft was at rest upon a mound-like outcropping of some dark pink lunar substance; beyond this, stretching far into the distance, the three Pennsylvanians saw a continuing gentle slope of far paler material, nearly white in tint.

Professor Thintwhistle leaped the short distance from the portal of the ship to the pink surface upon which it now rested, carrying with him the canvas-covered implement. Herkimer followed him to the lunar surface, as finally did Jefferson Jackson Clay, the latter inadvertently uttering the first words ever spoken by earthmen upon the surface of the moon: "Boss, y'all sure dis ain't Pennsylvania?"

The blackamoor's query was met with a furious glare from the gray-haired *savant*, who proceeded to strip the canvas covering from the object which he had removed from the cupboard beside the *Arthur's*

main port. In a trice it was revealed—a lengthy portable flagpole, miniature gilt eagle at its top, bullet-
shaped metal point at its base, Old Glory attached
proudly, its forty-six stars and thirteen stripes reflecting old Sol's effulgence brilliantly in the clear lunar
day and the puce and cerice Buffalo Falls Normal
School pennon flapping beneath the national emblem.

"Stand you now one to either side," the Professor
told his two helpers. "Now," he continued, holding
aloft the metal-tipped flagstaff, "in the name of Chester Alan Arthur of Fairfield, Vermont, twenty-first
President of the United States of America and stalwart
Republican, and in the names of the Commonwealth
of Pennsylvania, Potawatamy County and the Buffalo
Falls Normal School, I claim this territory!"

So saying he plunged the metal base of the flagstaff
into the pink surface upon which they stood. For a
moment the surface rippled. "Steady now, lads," the
Professor adjured, thinking the while, *My gracious!
What strangely yielding material the moon is made of!*

Suddenly a great voice was heard from the sky. It
filled the ears of the three lunar argonauts, penetrating
easily Herkimer's ear muffs and Jefferson's flannel
flaps, rebounded from the skin of the *Arthur* and re-
verberated off distant hills and rock walls.

"God damn it!" the voice said in a deep but wholly
feminine contralto pitch, "Something just stung me
right on the nipple!"

For behold, reader, the intrepid little *Chester Alan
Arthur* had made ground upon the moon fairly
enough—but not upon the pumicey rocks that make
up the lunar surface itself. Nay, though delicacy be offended, accuracy of reportage must needs take priority
as we see that the plucky ether-craft rested precariously upon the lacteal faucet of a giant woman, to

whom the *Arthur* and her crew were no greater in scale than would be a bumble bee and three gnats to an earthly person!

With agility surprising for one of his advanced years the Professor scrambled up a ladder on the side of the *Arthur* and stood surveying the surprising landing field upon which she stood. The giantess, from whose massive vocal apparatus there was now emitting a deep-throated "grrrrr" lay basking upon the lunar rocks in the balmy rays of old Sol. She was as innocent of clothing as the day of her nativity, but there rose from her neatly-bobbed hair twin curling feathers that gave back the rays of the sun in flowing colors of green, red, gold and blue. Upon her forehead there depended a ruby of unsurpassed fineness and hue—to the giantess a mere bauble, to the earthly intruders upon her lunar domain it was the size of a half-grown black bear.

A chain of massive golden links hung about her neck, at its end a sigil of unknown significance and incalculable value rested between the twin hillocks upon one of which the ether-flyer had its momentary resting place. A serpentine bangle was clasped upon one massive arm, and an emerald of incomparable beauty decorated her navel.

While Professor Thintwhistle stood paralyzed with astonishment atop his sturdy craft he saw the massive lips of the giantess move once again into an angry grimace. She began to draw herself up onto her elbows, and as she did so she spoke once again. "What pest is this," she demanded, "that dares disturb the comfort of Selena, the Queen of the Moon?"

(Author's note: the proper pronunciation of the Queen's name is Suh-*lee*-nuh. Say it right!)

The Professor was nearly bowled off his feet at the

blast of air carrying these words from the lips of the giant queen; in all likelihood it was only the sparseness of the lunar atmosphere that saved him from a fate of tumbling and probable injury; as it was he clung for the moment to the stacks of the *Arthur*, then scrambled rapidly down the ladder once more and raced to the dumbfounded Herkimer and Jefferson.

"Now, lads," he exploded, "we seem to have landed in an inopportune locale. I think we would be wise to, *ahem*, pull up stakes if I may be permitted a tension-relieving witticism under the circumstances, and remove ourselves, our flagstaff, and our ether-flying craft to some location more stable than the present one."

"But, Professor," replied Herkimer with tears in his eyes, "we just got here. Must we leave so precipitously?"

"Lad, lad," the pedagogue responded sympathetically, "know you not that I wish as fervently as you to explore the surface of the moon? But we have landed upon . . . upon . . ." *How, delicately, can I inform this dolt?* the Professor wondered.

"Yes, sir, upon . . . what?" inquired the lad.

"Upon, ah, ahem," the Professor answered. "Well then, to be totally blunt about it, Herkimer dear, we have landed upon the, *ahem*, the *bosom* of a very large person of the female persuasion. Do you catch the drift of my words?"

The while this conversation was taking place the "ground" beneath the *Arthur* and upon which stood the three earthly visitors gave evidence of undulations, at first barely noticeable, but of increasing vigor and persistence, until the three explorers found it needful to clutch at one another and to cling to their flagstaff for support in order to retain control of their feet, and the ether-flyer itself began to rock to and fro with the violence of the upheavals.

Without warning the surface upon which all stood shifted, as it would were Selena to rise from her reclining posture to an upright position.

"What is befalling us?" cried Herkimer.

"Lawsa marcy!" quaked the knock-kneed Jefferson.

"There's no time to bandy words," ejaculated Professor Thintwhistle. " 'Tis a time for quick action, not lengthy conference. Quickly, lads, get yourselves back into the *Arthur* and prepare for a quick resumption of our flight!"

While the two younger fellows spun on their heels and made for the hatchway of the ether-flyer the Professor remained clinging perilously to the flagstaff which he had so confidently planted but a few moments before in the yielding pink surface upon which they had landed. *The lady is angered, as well might she be,* mentated he. *To make some small amends it would be well at least to remove the barb from her tender and offended being.*

So thinking he knelt upon one knee and seized the flagstaff with both his blunt but sturdy hands. Gripping his infamous cracked briar in his large teeth as if to draw from it added strength, he drew up the flagstaff in a single mighty heave. With a loud *shloof-pop* it exited from the pinkish surface in which it had been buried, and nearly flew out of the pedagogue's powerful grasp. It was as if the staff had been pushed from within the giantess's form as it was pulled out by the intruder.

"Ah, and so to safer ground!" cried Professor Thintwhistle as he followed his two subordinates, racing across the pliable surface toward the port of the courageous little craft in which they had made the long journey from earth.

Reaching the *Arthur*'s main port a mere few strides behind Herkimer and Jefferson, the Professor found the hatchway closed and locked from within. He pounded upon it with the flagstaff and threatened to smash in an isinglass window with the staff if they did not admit him, upon which the hatch was opened and eager hands dragged the now trembling *savant* within the ether-flyer.

"Why did you fellows lock me out?" panted the Professor in nearly breathless tones.

"We thought you were lost," responded Herkimer. "We are so pleased that you are with us again!"

Professor Thintwhistle surveyed the cabin. Where Herkimer had burst in there was Cleopatra's bowl overturned while the feline mother stood complaining at the intrusion. Herkimer stood, his skimmer dangling at the end of its elastic cord, his ear muffs set askew and dangling from his neck.

Jefferson Jackson Clay was kneeling in supplication, beads of perspiration mingling with tears upon his dusky cheeks.

Professor Thintwhistle, cracked briar clenched in his square-cut canines and fists angrily planted upon Mackinaw-clad hips, glowered at the two. He wasted no time in recriminations, however, for the tremors which marked Selena's angry breathing and the shifts of attitude which reflected her movements from a horizontal to a vertical posture, were sending the *Arthur* shaking and tumbling about.

With a crispness of command based on long experience in dealing with boys at the Buffalo Falls Normal School, the Professor barked a series of commands to the two distressed persons who stood now in the center of the saloon between the portrait of Zaghlul Pasha and another opposite, that of "Old Tut's" own Old Dad, Thaddeus Unganno Thintwhistle. "Quickly, boys, prepare her for a new flight!"

Herkimer proceeded to batten potentially dangerous objects into place, and to tend to the delicate Cleopatra and her brood, while Jefferson Jackson Clay hied himself to the boiler room, there to stoke up the mighty steam engines of the *Arthur* with that fine black anthracite coal for which the Potawatamy County country of western Pennsylvania is so justly famed.

While the two subordinate ether sailors were thus engaged, the captain of the courageous little craft had hastened to his own duty station on the Captain's Veranda, and was doing all needful to prepare the ship once more to rise.

He reamed out the magneto, slipped the clutch in and out of position, ran the gear lever through its several settings, examined dials and meters, flexed levers, *hallooed* back to Jefferson to ascertain that a full head of steam was up, and just before casting off he looked with gimlet eyes through the isinglass curtain before the steering wheel.

Where the metal-tipped flagstaff had been planted and then so precipitately removed, a small pock-mark had been left in the dark pink surface. Now it had grown larger, and "Old Tut" could see a stream of rainbow-tinted air escaping from the hole, first pink, then red, then purple, then blue, a fresh burst with each ripple of the skin of the lunar giantess.

At the same time the opening itself, initially no farther across than the base of the flagpole, a mere inch or two, had grown and had changed from a simple puncture into a fissure that became increasingly elongated before the very eyes of the Pennsylvanian savant. *What would my Old Dad do in a situation like this,* the Professor wondered.

He held his bulging cranium with both his strong, calloused hands, and examined once more the control panel before him, noting with particular interest the steam pressure gauge, which, although it was steadily rising in level, indicated that as yet the pressure within the *Arthur*'s tanks was insufficient to raise the plucky craft into the thin air of earth's frigid companion.

He seized a flexible speaking tube which depended from the rococo ceiling of the Captain's Veranda and called into it, "What ho! Ahoy there in the boiler room! You, Jefferson, do you hear me?"

There followed a poignant pause during which the Professor turned to survey the saloon behind the Captain's Veranda. There in the cabin young Herkimer knelt beside Cleopatra, stroking her reassuringly while she in turn appeared to count and examine her kittens, assuring herself in the fashion of good mothers of all breeds and races that her offspring were accounted for and in good condition.

Above the scene the portraits of Zaghlul Pasha and Thaddeus Unganno Thintwhistle gazed unseeingly at each the other, for all the world as if they were engaged in a duel with their glances.

Again the Professor seized the speaking tube, glancing first out the port above his instrument panel and observing that the fissure in the soft surface upon which rested the *Chester Alan Arthur* was still growing by the moment.

From the giantess Selena no further word or sound had been heard following her enraged growl, but heavings and motions indicated that her ire was still aroused.

"Ho there, boiler room!" exploded the Professor into the speaking tube, "are you there you fool black man?"

After a pause of some duration there issued from the tube the voice of Jefferson Jackson Clay. "Ah's so busy shov'lin, pufessah, ah's hardly got time to talk!"

"Ah, well then, answer me but this, Jefferson: can you get her up to a higher head of steam, and quickly?"

"Ah's gwine 's fast 's ah can!"

"Well then, best give her a few more shovels full as quickly as you can, Jefferson, and then make for a safe spot as we are about to leave the presence of our unwilling hostess!"

He looked about once more, then said, "You too, Herkimer. We shall soon leave the surface once more, and you had best prepare yourself!"

With a final glance through the port, which revealed the fissure to have grown in length and breadth and to be advancing steadily in the very direction of the *Chester Alan Arthur* herself, the Professor gave a final shout of "Hold on!" and threw the gear lever into low.

The clutch went in with a boom, the drive train went into motion, powerful but under-pressure boilers giving every pound of force that they could. The propeller at the bow of the craft with the carven image of President Arthur for its spinner began to whirl in the thin lunar air.

The paddle wheels at either side of the *Chester A. Arthur* began slowly to revolve.

With a jolt and a lurch, black anthracite smoke bellowing from her twin smokestacks and gaslight providing a ghostly illumination to her darkened cabins, the *Arthur* began to creep forward across the epidermis of Selena the Queen of the Moon.

Barely in time, for as the *Arthur* crested the pink outcropping upon which it had perched so precariously since its landing, the gargantuan Selena drew herself to a fully upright posture. Had the *Arthur* remained in her former position she would now be tumbling end for end down a nearly vertical incline some hundreds of feet to the hard lunar soil below!

Instead the *Arthur* was moving forward across a small pinkish plain that dropped precipitously behind the ether flyer and that sloped away gradually to starboard as well as to port. Ahead the captain could see a pale wall rising and sloping away from the prow of the craft, with the growing fissure dead ahead.

And as the tinted gases continued to spew from the wound left where the Professor's flagpole had been first planted and then removed, the whole of the queen's epidermis seemed to be shrinking and shriveling away, while within the fissure itself Professor Thintwhistle's sharp eyes saw huge depths of darkness and strange lights and sights within!

With a frantic outcry of desperation the gray-haired *savant* shot home the controls to lift the *Arthur;* the sturdy ship responded as best she could, but lacking a full head of steam she rose but little, continuing her forward motion, bumped once again onto the pink convexity of Selena's shrinking form, screeched and rumbled ahead and pitched over entirely, into the blackness beyond.

"Hold tight, fellows," the Professor bellowed, "we are falling in, and what betides us now no one can foresee!"

CHAPTER 6
Some Surprises

Nor, indeed, could anyone have foreseen the astounding vision which awaited the three travelers as their little craft pitched over and fell into the fissure which had opened in the bosom of Selena the Queen of the Moon. What they might have anticipated, were they students of anatomy, would be a wound in the flesh of that giantess and a vision within of an intricate arrangement of muscle, blood vessels and nerves; even (were the wound but sufficiently deep) of bone. None of these did they behold.

Instead Professor Thintwhistle and his two youthful compatriots felt their courageous contrivance tumble stern-over-bow, carven propeller spinning and paddle wheels erratically revolving, into blackness and void. Streams of variously colored gases shot past them, vermilion, fuchsia, raw sienna, aquamarine, xanthic, buffeting the *Chester A. Arthur* as they made their way toward the opening made by the travelers' flagstaff at the moment of its unwise planting at the site of the *Arthur*'s landing.

Amazed at the sights they beheld, "Old Tut," Herk and Jeff clung each to a stanchion, staring aghast through the *Arthur*'s portholes. Even little Cleo, clutching anxiously to the sleeve of Herkimer's jacket,

uttered an amazed "meow" as she beheld that which
lay within the bosom of Selena the Queen of the Moon.

After a few astonished moments of silence the two
youngsters, Herkimer and Jefferson, burst into a bab-
ble of words.

"O Professor," ejaculated Herkimer, "what strange
place is this in which we find ourselves, and what is
the meaning of the sights which we behold?"

Jefferson, perspiring freely and trembling in his
every member, managed only to stammer a few incoherent phrases such as "Lawsy, lawsy . . . Ah sho' am
skyeered!" and his ever comical "Foots, do yo' duty!"
But there was nowhere that Jefferson's "foots" could
carry him now, that would return him to the safe and
secure workaday world he had left behind in the home
of Professor Theobald Uriah Thintwhistle of Buffalo
Falls.

Indeed not!

And it was the Professor himself who placed a
friendly and reassuring hand upon the shoulder of the
violently shaking darky, and said, "Ho, Jefferson, con-
tain yourself. What wonders we behold and what
perils we shall face ere we see again the green hills
and blue skies of our terrestrial globe we can but
guess. But in the meanwhile there is naught to be
gained by giving way to hysterics. Let us all remember that we are citizens of the Commonwealth
and of the United States, and let us not dishonor that
gentleman who sits in Washington and in whose name
we have attempted to stake our claim.

"All, then, to duty stations, and let us attempt to
right our craft and plot a course through these unknown ethers. Why look, let us take a lesson from little
Cleo!"

For the little mother had indeed crawled down from Herkimer's arms, and had returned to her duties with her babies, giving them that nourishment which a benevolent Nature provides, for all that each buffet and jolt of the craft tossed her and her offspring about most cruelly.

The captain and crew of the *Chester A. Arthur* directed their eyes and their attention to the courageous conduct of the cat mother and drew inspiration from the furry creature. The Professor turned back to the control panel on the Captain's Veranda, clutching his cracked and globuliferous briar in his round incisors, and began to adjust the many delicate controls there to be found.

Herkimer returned to the saloon, which was found to be in a state of sorry disarray, books tumbled from their shelves, pictures set all askew against the bulkhead walls, vases of blossoms tipped and smashed upon the Kermanshahan carpeting, and clumps of cat hair scattered here and there. The lad seized the initiative and began to restore the ship's saloon to its normal state of orderliness and decorum, straightening portraits, replacing books in their position (although stopping momentarily to examine the contents of a few), restoring blooms to their places within vases, and dumping accumulations of cat fur into waste baskets which stood beside each easy chair, along with smoking stands and antimacassar-covered end tables.

In the boiler room Jefferson Jackson Clay shucked his heavy lunar clothing and, clad only in britches and boots, his muscular black torso glinting with the perspiration of honest exertion, set to with his stoker's shovel, shoveling fine Pennsylvania anthracite into the ship's boiler, raising there a flame hotter and brighter even than that which a while before had consumed Leftenant Blithering-Snipe and his entire polyglot expeditionary force as well as their Doom Planetoid.

Before very much time had passed the *Arthur* had once again achieved a modicum of stability and orderliness. Her boiler was full, her smokestacks gave off a regular and reassuring *chuf-chuf-chuf*, her carven and polished propeller with its spinner bearing the portrait bust of her namesake whirled merrily through the intra-Selenate ether, her paddle wheels revolved with a steady surge of power.

Within the craft her captain clutched his cracked and oleogenous briar contentedly while he held her wheel on a steady forward course; Herkimer, having restored the main saloon to a semblance of normalcy, had come forward and seated himself respectfully upon the stairway leading from the saloon upward to the Captain's Veranda itself; and Jefferson Jackson Clay, whatever may have been his sinister thoughts at the moment, was at least outwardly dutiful in comportment and, having restored the boilers of the craft to full pressure and shoveled a full load of anthracite into the furnace, had donned proper livery and reported to his superiors for instructions.

Thus can it be seen that within the ether-flyer all was in order. But there remained to be dealt with the question of where the plucky craft ought to head.

Professor Thintwhistle turned to his two fellow travelers and advised them as follows: "Hold tight, fellows, while I run her through a series of maneuvers. Mayhap we can espy the opening through which we entered this extraordinary place, and head our craft back into the open lunar day."

Thus saying he tromped upon the clutch pedal,

shifted gears, flicked toggle switches and spun the little ship's steering wheel, placing the *Arthur* into a
series of intricate maneuvers, loops, spins, immelman
turns, dips, swoops and curves which would have been
the envy of any terrestrial swallow.

Throughout these ethereal acrobatics the three travelers and their little furry mascots clung bravely to
whatever support the *Arthur* offered. Their wondering
orbs beheld sights such as those never before witnessed by human observers. But nowhere saw they
any exit from their strange predicament.

At length the Professor restored the craft to a more
stable course of flight, dogged the steering wheel so
that he might more comfortably address his crew
without constant distraction, and turned to face Herkimer and Jefferson.

"Lads," quoth the *savant*, "I must urge you to buck
up and hold onto your courage. You, Herkimer, have
studied the lives of many a brave man, and you, Jefferson, I know have the simple-minded faith in divine
providence which is the sustenance of all your race.

"I must tell you fellows that the *Arthur* is lost in this
new void. But we are well supplied with food and
water, our craft has a plentitude of fuel, so you can see
that we are in no immediate danger.

"What we must do, then, is explore this strange
place, and in time I have confidence that we will indeed find our way out. In the meantime, all that is required is courage, diligent perserverence, and confidence in our Almighty Maker."

He then uttered a brief prayer, clenched cracked
and variolitic briar in his strong teeth, and turned
back to the wheel of the flyer.

Before the porthole of the *Arthur* there appeared a

panorama not wholly unlike that of the nighttime sky over Potawatamy County on an ordinary Midsummer's Eve. Ribbons of light in the sky showed the glow of distant gaseous clouds, nebulae and galaxies. Bright points gleaming steadily marked the positions of stars of many hues, reds, blues, yellows, greens and whites. Ribbons of colored gases continued to shoot by the ether-flyer, headed in every imaginable direction, propelled by no force which the Professor or his helpers could fathom.

At length the cabin of the *Arthur* was rent by a terrible *boom,* as of a volley of cannon. The three ether sailors ran to portholes at bow, starboard, and port of the craft, searching the black heavens in hopes of finding the source of the loud noise.

After but a moment's hesitation Herkimer exclaimed, "Professor, Jefferson, come and see what mine eyes behold!"

The others hastened to stand beside the youth at his isinglass-covered port and were astounded to see that which Herkimer had summoned them to observe.

"'Tis truly incredible!" exclaimed "Old Tut."

"Good golly Miss Molly!" moaned the blackamoor.

For floating upright in the invisible medium of the pervasive ether the three spatial argonauts beheld nothing less than a splendid Spanish galleon, its sails billowing as with an invisible sou'wester breeze, its anchors decked and its crew of Spaniards lining its rails, gesticulating excitedly and pointing at the *Chester Alan Arthur.*

The *boom* which had drawn the attention of the argonauts had been a hailing volley intended to do exactly that!

"Listen, lads," the Professor said, "they seem to be calling a message to us!"

The three ether sailors placed their ears to the isinglass curtain which filled the *Arthur*'s porthole and found themselves indeed greeted with a flurry of words.

"*Oye! Oye! Mira! Qué es eso? Qué pasa? Dónde estamos y a dónde va aquella cosa?*"

"What are they saying?" asked Herkimer, dumbfounded.

"Ho, lad," Professor Thintwhistle responded, "they are speaking the language of their homeland. Fortunately I studied languages as a mere stripling youth at the knee of mine own Old Dad and can translate for us now."

So saying he placed his ear carefully against the curtain once again, a look of rapt concentration filling his face. At length he turned again to the two others and said "They wish to parlay. Duty stations, chaps!"

In a trice the captain was again at his wheel, and the *Arthur* had begun to maneuver alongside the galleon, whose name, they could soon see painted in gilt letters upon her wooden hull, was the *Escarabajo de Plata*. The galleon's square-rigged sails stood bellied out, her pennons fluttering in the ethereal breeze. Before very long a small boat put out from her side, rowed by half a dozen rough-looking sailormen.

As soon as the *Escarabajo*'s boat fetched up against the hull of the *Chester Arthur*, Professor Thintwhistle dispatched Jefferson to the portal, adjuring him first to hold his breath for as long as the door was open, for, as the Professor explained in hopes that the servant might comprehend some fraction of his words, "We know not whether these Spaniards breathe air as do we, or the very ether of the void, and until we know, we must conserve our breaths until the door is again closed, lest we exhale good air and breath back in the cosmic ether which our lungs are unprepared to consume."

Obediently Jefferson made his way to the saloon door of the *Arthur* and opened it to admit an officer of the *Escarabajo*. The latterly indicated gentleman bowed graciously as he stepped into the saloon, doffing his feathered tricorn and handing it to Jefferson who ceremoniously deposited it upon an elk-antler rack beside the engraved portrait of Zaghlul Pasha.

The Spaniard was greeted courteously by Professor Thintwhistle, and delighted the latter personage by demonstrating an adequate, if highly accented, command of the English tongue. "I am Captain Juan Diego Salvador Jose Domingo de Lupe y Alvarado, commander of the royal galleon *Escarabajo de Plata*," he said with another bow to the Professor.

Professor Thintwhistle dispatched Jefferson for a tray of sherry, introduced Herkimer to the visitor, and suggested that they seat themselves about the deal-topped table in the saloon.

Captain Lupe quickly explained that the *Escarabajo de Plata* was the flagship of a small armada which had set out the previous April from a port in the nation of Spain. "The other ships were the *Piedras Volteandas* and the *Inquelina*. We were sailing in hopes of finding a new trade route to the Indies. Our men feared that we would fall off the edge of the world, and meet some dire fate—perhaps be crushed upon great rocks, or be devoured by serpents.

"After weeks of sailing marked by great privations of hunger and thirst, we heard a great roaring, as of a giant waterfall. Word was given to turn about, and all except the flagship were able to do so in time, but the

Escarabajo, being the farthest advanced, was swept over the edge into a giant abyss.

"As we fell, all commended our souls to the care of the angels, but instead of being dashed upon rocks or eaten by monsters, we found ourselves sailing this new sea. We have caught a few strange creatures for food, and passed through occasional rainstorms which have kept our barrels replenished but we cannot find our way. Perhaps you, a learned man, can offer us help."

So saying he looked hopefully to the Professor, but the latter turned his hands outward in a gesture he had many times taught to students of dramatic declamation in Buffalo Falls, and indicated that the *Arthur* was similarly distressed.

"Well," said Captain Lupe y Alvarado, "since we are in similar straits, should we find our way home first we shall try to keep track of the rescue route and send help for you, Professor."

"My thought exactly, Captain," replied Professor Thintwhistle. "We shall do the same."

At the completion of this agreement the two commanders quaffed what remained of their sherry and began to make their way back to the doorway through which Captain Lupe y Alvarado had entered the *Arthur*. Captain Lupe extended his hand to Jefferson, who placed in it the captain's hat, now neatly blocked and brushed.

Captain Lupe said to Jefferson, "*Muchas gracias, muchacho*," and accepted his headpiece back. He shook hands ceremoniously with Professor Thintwhistle, Captain Lupe's eye swept the interior of his hat; he gave no sign of noticing the message indited upon the ship's stationery of the *Chester Alan Arthur*, but placed his hat squarely upon his Spanish head and turned to make his exit.

Professor Thintwhistle said, "By the way, Captain Lupe y Alvarado, do you recall what year it was that you left Spain for the Indies?"

Captain Lupe scratched himself behind one Spanish ear, a look of puzzled concentration passing across his swarthy Iberian countenance. He put his hands on his hips and leaned backward as he pondered the Professor's question.

"Let me see now," he said (in Spanish for the moment, then switching back to English), "it was the twelfth year of the reigns of their Hispanic Majesties the Tsar Isidro and the Tsarina Fernanda. That would make the year, *mmm*, I believe anno domini 1492."

An expression of extreme startlement was the response which this statement elicited from Professor Thintwhistle. At length he was able to stammer "Are you certain?"

"Certain?" replied Captain Lupe y Alvarado. "Certain of what?"

"Why, ah . . ." Professor Thintwhistle dropped his cracked and incredulous briar in astonishment. "Why of, ah, the names of your monarchs. Did you not say Isidro and Fernanda?"

"Of course I did," replied the Spaniard. "Those are their names, what else should I tell you they are?"

"You are sure that they are not reversed—Ferdinand and Isabella?"

"Absolutely not!"

"And . . . and the titles you gave them, Tsar and Tsarina. Should they not be . . . that is, do you not mean King and Queen?"

"King, Emperor, Kaiser, 'tis all the same, is it not?" asked Captain Lupe. "But in Spain we use the form

Tsar and Tsarina, as we have for nearly five hundred years, since the Muscovites helped us to crush the Moors in 1000 A.D."

"My, my, my," mumbled Professor Thintwhistle around the stem of his briar, which he had recovered and placed firmly between his teeth once again, "this will require much deep thought. And tell me, sir," he went on, brightening, "how long has it been since you sailed from your home port?"

Again the Spaniard scratched himself, still standing in the closed doorway of the *Chester Alan Arthur*. "Of that I am not so utterly certain," he said. "I know that we sailed in the spring of the year 1492. It was not long after that that we met our fate of being carried over the great waterfall."

"Well, what year do you think it is now?" asked the Professor.

"Is it not still 1492?" asked Captain Lupe.

The Professor shook his head, as if relishing a choice jest at the expense of some faculty fellow at the Buffalo Falls Normal School.

"Could it be that it is already 1493?" asked the captain.

Again the Professor shook his head in indication of a negative reply.

"Well then what year is it?" demanded the captain.

"My dear sir," Professor Thintwhistle responded, "my companions and I left the village of Buffalo Falls in the Commonwealth of Pennsylvania—you have heard of Buffalo Falls, have you not?"

"I have not, sir," admitted the Spaniard.

"Of Pennsylvania?"

"No, sir."

"America, the New World, the United States?"

"No, no, no," replied the captain.

"Well, it matters not, then, but we left Buffalo Falls on the twenty-third day of May, 1884, a mere few days ago." He paused and stroked his beard thoughtfully while puffing at his briar in concentration until rings of blue smoke wreathed his gray and curly head.

At length he spoke once again. "That is," he went on, "I believe that it was but a mere few days ago!"

"I regret to state such a belief, Professor," the captain said, "but I am very much afraid that you are mad, sir, and I shall beg to take my leave of your madman's ship and return to the *Escarabajo de Plata*." So saying he made his exit to the small boat which had waited faithfully during the entire period of Captain Lupe y Alvarado's visit aboard the *Chester A. Arthur*.

"Hold breaths, lads!" commanded Professor Thintwhistle as the port was opened once again.

The Spaniard stepped from the saloon of the etherflyer onto the gunwales of his ship's small boat, and was conveyed back to the *Escarabajo de Plata,* waving his hand in friendly fashion all the while.

As Captain Lupe stepped back onto the deck of his galleon he might have been seen to remove his hat from his dark and curly head and examine its inside. He drew from it a piece of paper and examined it carefully, casting dark glances at the *Arthur*. At length he turned and disappeared into his cabin.

As the *Arthur* and the *Escarabajo de Plata* drew slowly apart, Jefferson Jackson Clay remained at the porthole beside the engraved portrait of Zaghlul Pasha in the main saloon of the ether-flyer, his eyes fixed on the slowly disappearing galleon. What thoughts passed through his mind during these moments were unknown to Professor T. and to Herkimer.

Had they but known the nature of those thoughts, the remainder of the voyage of their sturdy little craft had been far different from the events which were to follow!

CHAPTER 7
Activities in Several Places

The staunch commander of the ether-flyer *Chester Alan Arthur* turned to address his crew of two, removing his cracked briar from the staunch grip of his strong teeth and ruffling his graying locks in a characteristic gesture before uttering any syllable. For a brief moment his sharp but rheumy eyes darted from one sailor to the other, taking in the alert but brainless stare of Herkimer as well as the dull gaze of the cabin boy Jefferson.

At length Professor Thintwhistle exhaled a deep breath, then, pointing with his cracked briar through the isinglass-covered port in the direction in which the galleon *Escarabajo de Plata* had departed, he said, "Our Iberian friend has given me considerable to ponder, what with his tale of a Muscovite foray against the Moors, Spanish Tsars and Tsarinas, and particularly with the strange discrepancy in time implied by the date of departure which he claims.

"However," and at this point the pedagogue made a gesture of dismissal with his two chunky but powerful hands, "the Spaniards have taken their leave and, if you will pardon a schoolish play on words, having left us, leave us no particular assurance of aid, for all that I am certain that the captain will honor his pledge should his ship find its way back to Europe.

"Nevertheless, in the meantime we must needs shift for ourselves. It is good news that food and water are available in this strange ethereal ocean, and Jefferson, if you will keep an eye on the level of our anthracite stock we shall keep watch for driftwood to keep your boilers hot after our coal is exhausted.

"As for the present time, lacking both chart and landmark as we are, let us pluck up our spirits and regard our present predicament as a heaven-sent opportunity to set forth on an expedition of discovery, and prepare ourselves to astonish the fall convocation of the Buffalo Falls Normal School Scientific Society with a full and documented report of our findings!

"And for the moment, let us fortify ourselves with a slight repast of petit fours and ginger beer. Jefferson, will you do the honors please?"

So saying the Professor bowed gravely to the African houseman who, much to the amusement of the onlooking Herkimer, returned the courtesy in his typically oafish and clumsy manner, and exited to the pantry in order to carry out his instructions.

While this pleasant little ceremony was taking place deep in the unknown void which the *Arthur* had entered by way of the inadvertently administered wound in the bosom of Selena the Queen of the Moon, let us briefly turn our eyes elsewhere, to the comfortable if slightly antique quarters of the Faculty Club of the Buffalo Falls Normal School.

At the moment of our unobserved arrival there were present in the sitting room of the Faculty Club but four persons: Mr. Pinchard, a tall and painfully thin master of mathematics; Miss Taphammer, a daringly advanced feminist who had triumphed in her struggle to be permitted to teach music to the students of Buffalo Falls; the Rev. Goodspeed, pastor of the Buffalo Falls Straight Gospel Congregation and president of the Potawatamy County Ministerial Alliance; and the jolly, rotund Mr. Blount, geography master and a great favorite with faculty and students alike.

It should be noted, of course, that the Rev. Goodspeed was a guest in the confines of the Faculty Club, being a member of the Buffalo Falls School Board and *ex officio* privy to the activities of the school's staff.

At this moment, late in the afternoon following the departure of the institution's students for the day, the four persons assembled in the club room were discussing the most sensational occurrence to transpire in the town since the dedication of the Union War Memorial some eighteen years earlier.

Mr. Pinchard, the mathematics master, was at this moment holding forth on the topic of the disappearance of Professor Thintwhistle. "I have always held that a man of such unconventional views must come to an ill fate," said Mr. Pinchard. "To hold the views which Thintwhistle does, even in private, should, in my opinion—which I will make so bold as to express in mixed company—" and he offered a curt nod to Miss Taphammer, whose presence on the faculty of the Normal School he had vigorously opposed, "alone disqualify him from a position in which he molds the characters of the young.

"But not only does the miscreant hold his unconventional views, he makes so bold as to express them to his very students! To think, Reverend," and he made a half-bow in the direction of Mr. Goodspeed, "Professor Thintwhistle accepts the foul and blasphemous views of the wicked Darwin, claiming that we are all descended from the beasts.

"Why, my sainted forebears must whirl in their graves at the utterances of such a man. And he seeks support from the likes of the apostate Bishop Brown of Ohio!"

Grim-visaged and serious of tone, the clergyman nodded agreement with the views of the mathematician. "Such a person calls down upon himself the wrath of heaven. But you know, of course, my dear Pinchard, that William Montgomery Brown—I will not grant him the courtesy of a title which he has dishonored and of which he has been stripped—has been branded a heretic, as much for his Bolshevist social ideas as for his evolutionist scientific theories.

"He has been read out of the House of Bishops, removed from the rolls of the church, and banished to the outer darkness. Such a fate may well lie in the future of Professor Thintwhistle, at a forthcoming meeting of the Buffalo Falls School Board, of which, as you know, I am a leading and influential member!"

So saying the clergyman lapsed into grim and angry silence.

"But, gentlemen," put in Miss Taphammer, "is no one concerned that misfortune has overcome the Professor? After his disappearance the town's small children had been heard to remark upon the curious sight of 'Old Tut' proceeding toward Revolutionary Hill in an unconventional vehicle and in the presence of the boy Herkimer and the Professor's servant Clay."

"Madam," responded Mr. Pinchard in his most severe tone, "as far as I am concerned it is a case of good riddance to bad rubbish, and I should be delighted never again to lay eyes upon the old heretic or any of his associates, be they student, servant, or—" and here he snickered an evil-sounding snicker—"music mistress."

The Rev. Goodspeed joined in Mr. Pinchard's un-friendly sneer, but the rotund geographer Mr. Blount interceded by saying, "I am sure, Pinchard old fellow, that you mean to make no improper suggestion."

But Miss Taphammer, her feminine ire now roused, refused to accept the implied soothing of Mr. Blount's words. "Mr. Pinchard," she hissed angrily, "I make no pretense of hiding my high regard for the courage and honesty of character of Professor Thintwhistle, howev-er unconventional his views. It was he, you will recall, who championed my application for the position which I presently hold, and succeeded in overcoming the prejudice of certain persons present in this room against members of my sex.

"If there is no spark of human compassion within your narrow niggardly breast, Mr. Pinchard, nor Christian charity in the heart of a supposed man of God, Rev. Goodspeed, I shall be delighted to leave the precincts of this club and make my way to the home of Professor Thintwhistle in hopes of uncovering some clew as to the whereabouts of the three disappeared persons. For all we know they are in dire need of as-sistance."

She turned at this juncture to the rotund and good-natured Mr. Blount and said, "Sir, as a geographer and as the only true gentleman present, will you be so good as to accompany me to the Thintwhistle domi-cile, where we may proceed to investigate the mysteri-ous disappearance of the three absent persons?"

Before the astonished Pinchard and Goodspeed could find voice to contradict the harsh words of the angered Miss Taphammer, the lady had seized Mr. Blount by the arm and marched with a snort from the room!

At the same time that the angry Miss Taphammer and the accommodating Mr. Blount were making their way from the precincts of the faculty club to the locale of the Thintwhistle home in hopes of uncovering the whereabouts of professor, student, and servant, those three intrepid travelers were gaily munching ladies' fingers and napoleons, quaffed down with foaming mugs of dark ginger beer in the saloon of the *Chester Alan Arthur.*

The controls were dogged so that the craft proceeded on a steady course without need of human intervention while the furnace beneath her boilers was stoked to a brightness that would need no replenishment for some while.

In the saloon, neath the watchful eye of the portrait of Zaghlul Pasha the three explorers were seated, the Professor in a velvet-cushioned Morris chair, his elbow comfortably placed on the antimacassar covering a deal-topped table, a half-filled glass in one hand, the other raised in dramatic gesture as he outlined the splendid opportunities ahead for the *Arthur* and her crew.

Herkimer sat in a simple curved-wood rocker nearby, drinking in every word of the elderly *savant,* whose cracked briar rested, for the moment forgotten, in a cut-glass ashtray near his elbow.

And the blackamoor Jefferson Jackson Clay had been permitted, in the spirit of camaraderie of the moment, to seat himself upon the Kermanshahan carpet at the feet of Professor Thintwhistle, from which point of vantage he listened, with all *outward* signs of respect, to the peroration issuing from the bearded *savant* before him.

"We know not," the Professor was saying, "what

strange new starry space we have entered. The extent
of the universal ether may indeed be infinite. If this be
so, then there need be no limit whatever to the
number of stars and universes, planetoids and comets,
unprecedented phenomena, strange creatures, undis-
covered races, peoples, nations and civilizations yet to
be discovered.

"It is this great opportunity which has been opened
to us.

"How we came to the new ether through the wound
in the great lady of the moon we know not either, but
to all signs this strange interior world is far larger than
the inside of one person, even though that person happen to be a giantess.

"Nor can we guess what other earthly travelers may
have found their way, by one route or another, to this
strange place. If the galleon *Escarabajo* found its way
here, having first passed over a mammoth waterfall,
while we ourselves entered by way of the lunar giantess' bosom, what other means of access to this place
may there not be? And indeed, what means of egress
herefrom?"

So saying he swept the two younger persons, Herkimer and Jefferson, with his steely gaze.

"Perhaps we will encounter the ten lost tribes of
Israel," the Professor went on, "or meet the missing
crew of the *Marie Celeste*. Who knows but that we
shall uncover the hidden abode to which Lilith re-
treated before the creation of Eve. Or that we shall
find the lost children of the town of Hamelin in
Germany."

His eyes grew misty and his tone introspective as
the Professor continued to catalog the many wonders
which might lie ahead, the many mysteries which it

might be the fate of the *Arthur* to unravel. At length
he shook his steel-tinted leonine locks and smiled be-
nevolently at his two helpers.

"Well then, lads," he concluded, "as you can see it is
a matter of golden opportunity which lies ahead of us.
We need but keep up our courage, refuse to quail in
the face of adversity, stick together in this our great
quest, and we will yet return to Buffalo Falls covered
with glory!

"To our stations, then, and let us see what grand adventure lies ahead of us on some new world in the
ether!"

So saying he flung down the last of his ginger beer,
licked the sweet icing of a final napoleon from the
thick and sturdy fingers of one hand, replaced his
cracked and catoptrical briar between his large pre-
molars and, giving the boy Herkimer an enigmatic
glance, strode purposefully once more to the Captain's
Veranda, there to undog the controls of the ether-flyer
and cast a watchful eye through the port before him,
searching out the course to be followed by the little
ship.

Herkimer seized pencil and paper and, stationing
himself at another porthole in the saloon, prepared to
sketch the new heavens as they appeared at this particular place.

Jefferson tidied up the section of the saloon in
which they had shared their snack, and disappeared
sternward, carrying the debris of the repast with him
on a precariously balanced tray, shuffling his large and
widely splayed feet in a little dance step he had been
working on and whistling a gay if discordant tune, one
greatly reminiscent of his earlier song, "Eat dat chick-
en pie!"

Other thoughts occupied his brain, which was supplied with a cunning, if sinister, intelligence which would have surprised the ordinary observer of the Caucasian race.

Meanwhile, on the surface of the moon, which had passed from the view of the three intrepid Pennsylvanians at the moment that their little craft dipped over the edge of the fissure in the bosom of Selena the Queen of the Moon, that very lady was faced with a problem of her own, which she was shortly to set about solving in a manner uniquely her own.

Let us leave the crew of the *Arthur* to their own devices, just as we have left the occupants of the Buffalo Falls Normal School faculty club room to their own means; it is for each of us to work out his or her own destiny, and when sufficient time has passed for each of the parties to have advanced their respective destinies sufficiently to warrant our renewed attention, they shall assuredly have it.

In the meanwhile, let us turn our eyes and our thoughts back to the gargantuan Selena. Indeed this lady warrants our attention, for she presents a most striking and imposing aspect to the observing eye.

Her hair, from which twin curving peacock feathers rise colorfully, is itself of a rich and lustrous Titian tint, its deep tones set off by the ruby which reposes upon her broad and furrowless brow. Her complexion is of a perfect smoothness and the beauty of her countenance is unmarred by blemish. Her eyes are a dark green in tone, and her pale skin, a pinkish white to the first glance, reveals a slight overtone of verdure.

Her form is exquisite for all its massive dimensions, and the amulet worn on the chain about her neck catches the sunlight and reflects as would a badge of carven gems.

But the graceful bosom of the lady shows marked

signs of shrivelling as puffs of colored gas continue to hiss, now slowly, from the wound caused by the inadvertent eagerness of her three brief visitors from the terrestrial orb.

Indeed, as Selena directs her gaze downward to her own graceful form she is horrified to see that she is shrinking and shrivelling by the moment. Indeed, with each hiss of red gas her shoulders seem to grow more narrow, with each jet of escaping yellow her gracefully curved belly grows smaller, with each burst of violet her bosom reverts to the former flatness of the young girl, with each puff of blue, of green, of pink, of brown, of gray she finds herself becoming less and less the impressive figure of the past.

She casts her glance about her in alarm. She stands now where she had formerly bathed in the friendly rays of old Sol upon a smooth bit of lunar rock. Before her she espies grassy lawns and a moon garden of wondrous plants pruned and shaped by the gardeners of the royal court into fantastic shapes: demons and dragons, beasts and beauties, ships and carriages, horses, dogs, lions, whales, swordfish; portrait busts of great lunar rulers and visitors of the past—Cyrano, Bishop Godwin, the voyagers of Lucian's history; reptiles and butterflies and dancers and athletes.

The beauteous Queen runs down pathways of scarlet and xanthic blossoms, her naked feet fairly flying over the bluesward trails that separate the rows of plants.

At length the garden ends, giving upon a moat the bridge of which Selena clears in a few flying bounds. She now dashes across an open field where the Royal Household Ice Cream Brigade is drilling for the grand anniversary parade and orgy to be held upon the occasion of the next full earth.

The troopers stand in amazement as their unquestioned monarch and the queen, as well, of their affec-
tions, sprints past, hardly noting their presence nor
their precision maneuvers; one young trooper in fact is
seen to drop his ice cream upon the lactiphageous carpet of the parade ground, where it is promptly devoured, the tiny blossoms of lacteophage murmuring sighs
of joy and contentment as the Ice Cream Brigadesman
returns in disgrace to the quartermaster for a replenishment of his supply.

Selena reached the portico of her official residence,
the Palace of Peace and Joy, which stands in ocean-
green splendor, flinging its spires and minarets into
the black lunar sky, an edifice the beauty of which is
known throughout the lunar orb and which is visited
by pilgrim devotees of grace the year around, most
particularly upon the occasions of the full earth.

Royal guardsmen clad in snowy white and scarlet
turbans and breech-clouts spring to attention as their
sovereign passes fleetingly up the front steps of the
Palace of Peace and Joy. They gasp and fall to whispered converse as Selena passes.

"Is her majesty well today?" asks Touggourt, brushing his moustache back from his mouth as he speaks.

"She seemed somehow smaller than usual," answers
Sulawesi, a gem falling from his turban at the violent
shake of his head. He removes the turban to replace
the gem.

"Did you not hear a hiss as she passed?" inquires
Chemulpo with a puzzled look on his face.

"I could swear that the atmosphere took on a
strange color just after she passed," avers Aguascalientes.

"And that a beautiful perfume which I never before

smelled lingers behind her majesty," adds Zartaclave tapping his nose with a long and bony finger.

Yet within the Palace of Peace and Joy Queen Selena waits for no comments, stops to visit with no one. She is growing visibly smaller, the distance from the crown of her head to the ceiling becomes greater with each passing moment, the strides which she so bravely takes become shorter and painfully shorter.

With gracefully tapering fingers she holds closed the wound in her bosom through which her inner self is slowly escaping, until she reaches the royal apartments, flings up the lid of an intricately carven chest, rummages through its contents and emerges at last with a small coffer which she lays carefully upon the top of the chest.

The beauteous Selena opens the coffer, lifts out a shallow tray and from the compartment beneath extracts a flexible, transparent tube the length of her forearm.

She places one end of the flexible tube between her soft and gracefully curved lips. The other she affixes to the point on her bosom where first the tip of the explorers' flagstaff punctured her fair skin, holding the rend closed about it. Holding the two ends of the tube in place, Selena delivers a terrific breath of the lunar atmosphere through the tube, into her bosom, which swells slightly at the arrival of new substance.

Selena blows, grows, blows, grows, perspiration dotting her creamy brow, concentration filling her handsome face, continuing to reinflate her gargantuan form until, satisified that she has regained her full stature she holds shut the wound in her bosom, extracts from the coffer before her a tube of quick-setting cement, and reseals the rend in her epidermis.

Now she puts away the tubes, that used to transmit lunar air and that containing the cement, and lies down briefly to give her wound a chance to dry and heal.

Her kingdom has had a close call this day!

CHAPTER 8
Into an Inner World

Let us return our attention to the occupants of the ether-flyer *Chester Alan Arthur*. The Professor and captain of the craft stands his watch upon the Captain's Veranda, cracked briar clenched in large teeth, brass buttons gleaming upon his naval uniform, curls of steely gray streaming from his scalp and cheeks alike, piercing gaze fixed upon the new universe beyond the isinglass portholes of his plucky hand-crafted vehicle. He clutches the steering-wheel of the *Arthur* in large and capable hands, feet planted firmly on the polished planks of the floor of the Veranda. The sights he beholds are such as have been seen by the commander of no ship in the known history of the earth.

Behind the Captain's Veranda, down a short flight of steps in the Kermanshahan-carpeted and mahogany-decorated saloon of the ship Herkimer sat beside a window of his own, his innocent and boyish gaze fixed equally upon the wonders beyond the sturdy hull of the *Arthur*, a pad of pink foolscap upon his knee, stylus in hand, busily sketching and labeling portrayals of the wonders of this inner ether, the first map to be made of this new territory.

And farther still to the rear of the *Arthur*, behind

closed and bolted doors in the service area of the ship, was Jefferson Jackson Clay. He had stoked up the boilers to a high degree of flame and now, freed of immediately pressing tasks, was pursuing matters of his own interest.

From the familiar roll-top desk which he unlocked with a cleverly disguised key Jefferson extracted a blank book of his own and, with a writing instrument of unusual and surprising nature, indited therein an inscription of enigmatic but foreboding significance:

> *From the Cabin Boy's Log, Ether Date 3208.94705:*
>
> The expedition of the ether-flyer continues to blunder from one near-disaster to another as incompetent honky pilot T and supercargo ofay nincompoop H perform as anticipated; i.e., idiotically.
>
> The *Chester Arthur* is wandering aimlessly while communication has been established with Captain L y A of the galleon *Escarabajo de Plata.* Further log entries will be made as opportunity permits.
>
> *Venceremos!*
>
> Clay, Cabin Boy

The African closed his notebook and twirled a combination lock which held its cover in place, then lodged the volume carefully in a dusty pigeon hole in the rear of the roll-top desk, slid his unusual writing instrument into a specially prepared holder, watched a tiny red eye wink out above the pigeonhole, winked back and gave the desk a playful dig in the slats, rolled down its top and locked the covering in place.

Chuckling evilly, the blackamoor turned away from the desk and straightened his serving man's livery. He glanced into a chipped and flaking looking glass, which once had graced the table of a lady of quality before being passed through the hands of a major domo to reach the service of such as he, and carefully resumed the mien of unintelligent servility which he habitually wore in the presence of the Professor and Herkimer.

Carefully selecting a filthy and infamous dust cloth from a row of hooks that rimmed the scullery door, Jefferson made his way back through the boiler room and pantry to the saloon of the ether-flyer. There he proceeded to feign his accustomed duties, slapping carelessly at bookshelf and tabletop, whistling gaily but flatly his familiar darky rhapsody to which even the innocent Herkimer began unconsciously to tap one neatly broganned foot: "Eat dat chicken, eat dat chicken pie, oh my!"

Casually leaning over Herkimer to take an ineffectual swipe at the isinglass that filled the window frame above the boy's neatly parted head, Jefferson took quick note of the contents of Herkimer's foolscap pad.

There he espied a crude sketch of the Spanish galleon *Escarabajo de Plata* and a scrawled notation of the encounter with Captain Lupe y Alvarado, all clearly of no news to Jefferson. Slyly flipping to the next page Jefferson found a rough outline of a series of astronomical configurations, stars, comets and gas clouds such as he himself had seen through the scullery window a few moments earlier.

A third sheet of pink flimsy yielded the first surprise beheld by Jefferson—against the background of the intra-Selenate void there seemed to swim a human figure, emphatically feminine, with heavily accented features of torso and flowing hair, clad only in clinging wisps of diaphanous gossamer, an expression on her face, although crudely rendered, clearly intended to suggest a combination of languor and sensuousness.

With sudden force the pad of flimsy was wrenched from Jefferson's grasp and snapped vigorously to. In shrill and angry tones, his face scarlet with rage, Herkimer shouted, "Here, you darky pokeynose, give me that back!"

With difficulty suppressing a smirk Jefferson turned back to his task of wiping the isinglass window beside the engraved portrait of Zaghlul Pasha, whistling again his gay if simple tune, "Eat dat chicken, eat dat chicken pie, oh my!" and tittering frequently until poor Herkimer with tears of rage picked up his sketching utensil and trotted to the far side of the saloon cabin, stationing himself at the opposite porthole and presenting to the room only a scarlet back of the neck.

"Yowsah, yowsah!" mumbled Jefferson, scrubbing lackadaisically at a flyspeck that marred one edge of the window Herkimer had but recently abandoned. At the same time he glanced covertly about to assure himself that Professor Thintwhistle was fully occupied upon the Captain's Veranda, which indeed he was, and that Herkimer had not seen fit to turn away from the vista to which he had but newly attached himself.

Thus assured of momentary privacy at the least, Jefferson affixed his own murky orbs to the window nearest the portrait of Zaghlul Pasha, gazing with every indication of purpose into the starry void outside. Soon there swam within his purview an apparition the likes of which had never been seen on earth save in the religious fantasies of aborigine fanatics as yet unenlightened to the splendors of the divine message of the gentle Jesus.

A serpent, its body lengthy, slim, sinuously graceful, glided to a position beside the *Arthur*. Its length was astonishing, its head flat and spade-like in form and its xanthic eyes flashed an apparent intelligence of the most startling degree. Along its writhing flanks a series of small wings protruded, feathers in the most splendid of tints ruffling and again smoothing themselves with each twitch or bend of the powerful body.

At its dorsal extremity, in place of the customary epidermal point there appeared an astonishing sight: an octahedral globe of small transparent panes, lighted from within, and containing a gnome-like creature of sly and cynical demesne, clad all in a foresty green and wearing a serpent-feathered cap upon his cleverly shaped head.

As the feathered serpent slid hissing past the plucky ether-flyer the wily Jefferson reached into a vest pocket of his proper and neatly arranged livery and pulled forth a signalling device which he carefully attached to the inside of the isinglass. He began tapping at it as the tail of the serpent passed near the window, and as he did so the strange creature within the octahedral globe signalled back, tiny flashes of multichromatic light bearing a message of unknown content to the jubilant Clay.

In a moment the exchange was over and the ethereal flying serpent curvetted away from the *Arthur,* its tail-light extinguished, its strange passenger lost to sight in the darkness of the intra-Selenate space. As the serpent passed across the prow of the *Arthur* Professor Thintwhistle uttered a gasp of astonishment and called aloud "Herkimer! Jefferson! Attend me upon the Captain's Veranda!"

The two whom he addressed proceeded to obey, the one in all ignorance and innocent eagerness to comprehend the purpose of his superior's message, the other giving every pretense of being his usual oafish and lackadaisical self while secretly well aware of the sight which he was being called to behold and in fact far more knowledgeable of its true meaning than the commander who summoned him.

"Behold!" Professor Thintwhistle exclaimed "'Tis the legendary flying serpent of the Aztecs—or, oh my, was it the Incas? Are my faculties deserting me when I am but in the prime of my life? Well, it matters little, and anthropology was never my field." Thus he mumbled and muttered on until interrupted in his introspective ruminations by Herkimer.

"Surely you remember, sire, it was the Aztecs who decorated their temples in Yucatan with the image of the flying serpent!"

"Of course, of course!" responded the Professor with a resounding clearance of his throat. "The point is, lad, that such a creature as had ever before been regarded as the figment of pagan superstition, is gyring and gimballing before our very portholes. Look!" And with the command he pointed dramatically through the porthole above his own instrument panel.

"Marvelous," crooned Herkimer. "What tale of wonder shall I spin when next I visit the Buffalo Falls Young Men's Christian Association on a storyteller's night! Though others spin fictions, I shall dazzle the credulity of all with the literal record of this wondrous journey!"

Professor Thintwhistle puffed merrily at his cracked and oracular briar, and clapped the lad heartily upon the shoulder, the while slipping a fine maroon powder into the breast pocket of the young fellow's tweed while the latter, all unawares, gazed in rapture at the fast-disappearing apparition beyond the windows of the ether-flyer.

Jefferson, meanwhile, feigned awe and terror, falling to his neatly creased knees and beseeching the Professor to protect him from "Dat skeery great snake out dere."

Professor Thintwhistle spurned the darky with one heavy boot, snarling, "Control yourself, Jefferson, and try to behave in the calm and enlightened manner to which we have attempted for so long to accustom you!"

"Yowsah, boss!" sniveled the houseman, and gratefully wiped his streaming eyes on the *savant's* ornately decorated uniform cuff, adding a loud honk of his flat and primitive nose for good measure and mumbling incoherent expressions of gratitude.

"Now then," the Professor said, "let us resume our diligent perusal of the great blackness beyond our portals, in hopes of finding some clew to our whereabouts and a means of egress from our strange predicament, lest our wonderful discoveries be wasted by virtue of remaining unreported to the scientific community of our homeland!"

So saying he once more glued his perceptive orbs to the window above the controls, urging Herkimer and Jefferson to do likewise in the saloon, the one near the portrait of Zaghlul Pasha and the other beside that of the Professor's own Old Dad.

Hardly had they complied with this instruction when Herkimer cried out in a loud and boisterous voice, "Look yonder, if my recollection of your astronomy lecture is not at fault, we may be nearing our very sun and his family of worlds!"

The others joined him, jostling and cursing, to get a

clear view through the porthole beside the engraved portrait of Thaddeus Unganno Thintwhistle, a deceased gentleman whose likeness exhibited a startling similarity to that of the present Thintwhistle who, barring unsuspected alterations in the fabric of fate was apparently slated to be remembered as the last of the Thintwhistle line.

Finally knocking the clumsy Jefferson to the floor where he lay mumbling a mixture of apologies and African imprecations against the treatment he was receiving from his social betters, Professor Thintwhistle secured a clear view through Herkimer's portal, and, after several pregnant moments devoted to the close study of the vista presented therein, he grunted a deep-throated "Hmmph!"

Then stepping back from the porthole the better to emphasize his points, the Professor declaimed, "Sonny, you indeed recognize the general configuration of our everyday solar system, but you fail to discern the fine details which distinguish that one which you see below us from that in which we were all born and had our being until the present time.

"The sun you see is indeed a G-type medium-well-done gas articulate, but by mere naked-eye observation I would estimate its temperature to be at least some five to ten degrees warmer than Sol. Its planetary family, furthermore, is distinctly at odds with our own. Note that the innermost planet possesses both oceans and clouds, neither of which pertain to the solar Mercury, while the third planet, which occupies the orbit equivalent to that of our own world is a distinct orange in color while our dear old earth is a mottled blue, green and brown.

"There are, further, several distinct belts of planetoids rather than Sol's one, and a family of equally sized trinary planets such as exist nowhere in our home solar system.

"Herkimer . . . and you, too, Jefferson," he said, signing the cringing servitor to rise and rejoin the group, "you behold the first extrasolar family of planets ever seen by earthly eye. Come, I shall have the honor of naming that warm and pleasant star myself. Mayhap I may win the smiles of a lady whose warmth and pleasant disposition I have similarly admired for long.

"Yes, Herkimer, if you will be so good as to record the fact, I shall designate this newly discovered star, 'Taphammer.'"

At these words the youth industriously scribbled a note on the first clear sheet of his foolscap pad, hurriedly skipping by the portrait of his fantasy maiden as he did so.

"And now," the *savant* continued, "let us prepare to explore that friendly sun's family of planets, and see if there be any suitable for the *Arthur* to land upon, that we might thus refresh ourselves and, if possible, make the acquaintance of local residents and obtain from them succor from our present predicament."

So saying he returned to the Captain's Veranda, leaving Herkimer with his sketch pad of flimsy alone in the saloon and Jefferson Jackson Clay to return to his own duties in the rear of the ship.

The outermost planets of the sun Taphammer were quickly abandoned as far too large, vaporous and chilly for the *Arthur* to attempt even a brief landing, while the several planetoidal concentrations proved far too dangerously congested for such an attempt. That left Taphammer I, a pleasant enough looking planet; Taphammer III, whose appearance bore an in-

triguing resemblance to a giant ball of tangerine sherbet displayed against the black velvet of the void; and
Taphammer VI-VII-VIII, the worlds of trinary configuration, each of which displayed evidence of possessing oceans and gaseous envelopes, likely signs of
the possibility of life.

Professor Thintwhistle guided the *Chester Alan Arthur* skillfully through the Taphammer system, paral-
leling the famous plane of the ecliptic or solar equator,
and passing low through the sky of each world in turn.

As they skirted the atmosphere of Taphammer I
many figures were seen running excitedly about, waving objects at the *Arthur* and pointing devices at it
which produced no effect discernable by the ethereal
argonauts, but which produced the effect of convincing
the hardy explorers that the welcome which they might
anticipate upon that pleasant-looking world might be
of less than the desired degree of friendliness.

Taphammer III proved to be of so frigid a climate
that its inhabitants, to all outward appearances a race
of giant King Charles Spaniels, were forced to spend
all of their time struggling to keep warm. They were
blessed to live on a planet where food was no problem
(although Herkimer surmised aloud that a perpetual
diet of tangerine sherbet would soon prove cloying),
but their perennial struggle against the rigors of low
temperature had robbed them of any surplus energy
to devote to the building of a high civilization, and
they too were given the "go-by" by the *Chester Arthur.*

As the plucky craft exited from the frigid atmosphere of Taphammer III Professor Thintwhistle remarked to his assistants, "I wonder what tales the
intelligent canines of that globe will pass on to their
descendents of the strange apparition which they today

beheld in their sky! Mayhap we three will live in the myths of Taphammer III as inhabitants of a magical bird that appeared one day and soared through the sky, spewing trails of black ash behind and bellowing terribly as we passed."

On the *Arthur* flew, her boilers' steady *chuf-chuf-chuf* reverberating in homely fashion through the quarters of the craft. At eventide the three sailors foregathered for their nightly repast, a small *filet de boeuf* prepared by the skillful hand of Jefferson, preceded by a creamy *vichyssoise* with chives and generous portions of *paté de fois gras*.

The main course was accompanied by creamed pearl onions, broccoli in hollandaise, tiny roast potatoes (one of which, slightly blackened, drew a reprimand for its irregular configuration and hard texture), asparagus salad *à la russe*, and hot butter rolls.

The entirety was of course accompanied by a selection of appropriate and tasty wines, chilled or aired as needed, and followed by baked Alaska, Bristol cream and cigars, the last named temporarily displacing the Professor's customary cracked briar, and a small example of which was sampled with evident relish by the youthful and inexperienced Herkimer.

As Jefferson dutifully cleared the debris of the repast from the antimacassared deal-top table in the ship's saloon and retired to the pantry to carry out such post-prandial duties as were needful in the circumstances, and indeed to make himself a hearty repast of the bits and portions left undevoured by his two social betters, Professor Thintwhistle and Herkimer settled themselves for a final pleasant evening aboard the *Arthur* preparatory to their impending planetfall in the brightness of the morrow's dawn.

At the Professor's suggestion Herkimer set up the flyer's portable Edison Gramophone, winding its spring mechanism to the very sticking point and ceasing barely in time to prevent damage to the delicate machinery within. He then selected a wax cylinder of high cultural merit and placed it upon the revolving shaft beneath the machine's delicate needle.

As Herkimer once again seated himself opposite the Professor the delicate voice of Jenny Lind, the Swedish Nightingale, filled the saloon of the ether-flyer with the sweet strains of a ditty by the French composer Bizet. Tones of fiddles, horns and pianos and kettle drums joined that lovely human voice, and beatific smiles spread upon the faces of the two as they participated vicariously in the performance of the melody, Herkimer tapping one of Jeshaw Callister's best brogans in time to the steady rhythm, while Professor Thintwhistle used a left-over coffee spoon to conduct the performance of the phantom orchestra.

At the end of the piece Herkimer burst into enthusiastic applause, the while he basked in the approving smiles of his senior cohort. When at last Herkimer had quieted and awaited instructions as to the selection of the following cylinder, Professor Thintwhistle added his own salute by proclaiming, "That fellow is not half bad as a composer, considering that he is a mere frog!"

After many more hours of merriment the Professor rose from his place and paced to the rear of the saloon, where he pounded loudly upon the pantry door and shouted a warning to Jefferson to be up bright and early in the morning with a hearty breakfast for all, that they might properly fortify themselves for planet-fall. He then bade Herkimer a courteous good-night, glancing slyly from the corner of his eye as the lad stretched and yawned.

In a short time the *Arthur*'s lights were doused, her controls dogged, her boilers damped, and all aboard her presented the full semblance of peaceful slumber.

CHAPTER 9
Buffalo Falls Reprise

In every nation and age there have been those who
advocated equality of the sexes and those who have
opposed this notion, holding that the subjection of one
gender to the will and whim of the other was at least a
requisite condition of good order and human progress
and in all likelihood an arrangement dictated by the
will of heaven and violated only at the risk of divine
retribution.

Through most of history and in most lands this
question has been couched in the form of doubts as to
the equal or inferior status of members of the female
sex, although in certain cases, as that of the Xichtupan
Indians of northwestern Ecuador and the Galaya
tribesmen of subcentral New Guinea, it is the male sex
which has been held subject to the commands of the
female.

In the town of Buffalo Falls, as the spring of 1884
advanced, a splendid and blossoming May preparing
to doff its crown of blue and fleecy white in favor of a
balmy and robust June, the question of female rights
was a lively one. Already we have made the acquaintance of Miss Olivia Taphammer, that lady whose ap-
pointment to the faculty of the Buffalo Falls Normal
School in the position of music mistress had been so
vigorously although unsuccessfully opposed by certain

of the male members of the teaching staff and school board.

At this moment Miss Taphammer and the good-natured and rotund geographer Mr. Winchester Blount could be observed striding together from the Normal School faculty clubroom through the streets of the town toward the apparently abandoned domicile of Professor Thintwhistle. Of the two it was Miss Taphammer whose strides were the more purposeful and whose expression was the more determined.

Her male companion, despite the ostensible superiority of his sex, spoke out in a troubled and uncertain voice. "Are you wholly convinced, Miss Taphammer, of the propriety of our attempting to enter Professor Thintwhistle's home in this manner? Suppose he is indeed absent from his accustomed haunts? Will not tongues wag and heads nod knowingly at reports of our unconventional conduct?"

"Suppose our colleague's home has been invaded by ruffians and he and his serving person lie now battered and helpless?" was Miss Taphammer's rejoinder. "Suppose they are in need of assistance, which we would fail to provide through overparticularity with regard to the forms of public conduct? It is needful, my dear Winchester, to place the well-being of Professor Thintwhistle and Jefferson Clay above our concern for the tales of malicious gossips!"

Blushing at the familiarity of his female companion in the use of his given name, Mr. Winchester Blount pursued his doubts by adding, "What of the missing boy Herkimer? Ought we not to inquire at his home to determine whether his parents have discovered any clew as to his whereabouts?"

"That is a useful suggestion, Winchester, but as you may be aware, the boy doted particularly upon Theo-

bald Thintwhistle and in view of their simultaneous
disappearance from the academy and from the general
society of Potawatamy County, I feel assured that
when we find any of the three missing individuals we
shall have uncovered the whereabouts of all!"

"You are probably right," said Mr. Blount. "Still, it
would hardly please one to incur the further dis-
pleasure of Mr. Pinchard and Pastor Goodspeed." A
worried expression formed upon Mr. Blount's round
and mobile countenance. "I fear that the course of
moral and social propriety eludes me in the present
situation."

"Well, buck up, Chester, and be prepared to give
me a hand," Miss Taphammer said vigorously, "for as
you can see we have arrived at the gate of Professor
Thintwhistle's yard and a moment of truth is in all
likelihood near upon us!"

Mr. Blount's only response was an astonished gasp
as Miss Taphammer punctuated her words with a
solid if unladylike thump between his well-padded
shoulder blades that threatened to loosen his collar
button and send his celluloid collar skittering across
the smooth plank sidewalk.

Miss Taphammer quickly opened the gate latch with
her lengthy and competent fingers and, stepping
through into the Professor's yard, she pointed a taffeta
arm and graceful hand at Herkimer's abandoned velocipede. "There, you see?" she said in triumph, "it is
Herkimer's wheel, and no Herkimer anywhere to be
seen. Find the man and we shall find the boy, exactly
as I said."

Mr. Blount advanced into the yard and, spying the
small anthracite digging which Professor Thintwhistle
had initiated earlier, ran to its edge and knelt with
eyes roving the subterranean works. "Miss Tapham-

mer," he exclaimed, "come and see what I have discovered."

The music mistress obeyed and, having examined the mine for herself, said to the jolly geographer, "You are clearly possessed of a goodly power of observation, Winchester. I wonder if you think it would be premature to attempt to deduce the meaning of these subterranean activities."

"That I cannot do," Mr. Blount said. "Surely Professor Thintwhistle was not attempting to tunnel through the earth to China, for all that doing so has been a topic of some discussion of late. Perhaps—" and his eyes roved once again over the small tools, picks and weighing pans which littered the work site— "the Professor was attempting the extraction of minerals from the earth."

"Bravo!" cried Miss Taphammer. "Observation and deduction, as the Irish Dr. Doyle so well expresses it in his little tales, are the key to scientific investigation. Now indeed we may consider ourselves on the track of Professor Thintwhistle."

"Oh, well, well," replied Mr. Blount, "so it may be, but unless the Professor and Herkimer have been done to death by the savage houseboy of the former, and buried beneath this mine, I fail to see how we have advanced in the location of the missing individuals."

"Indeed, my dear Winchester, it is not impossible that the Professor and the lad have been dispatched by Jefferson Clay and buried here to dispose of the bodies. The abandoned wheel of the youth and the tools of the Professor would in fact suggest as much. Only one doubts that Jefferson would dig only shallowly and cover over the bodies of his victims, and then abandon the site.

"He is half savage but I think more wily than most

realize. He would either fill in the Professor's mine or dispose of the evidence of his crime elsewhere. Besides, consider the reports of the children who saw the three of them proceeding with an unusual contraption in the direction of Revolutionary Hill shortly before their common disappearance."

"Then where do you think they might be, Miss Taphammer?"

"I think it is too soon to tell. But I think we would do well to examine the interior of the Professor's house before making wild guesses."

So saying she strode determinedly up the flagstone path to the front steps of the house, climbed the steps and crossed the porch. With the knuckles of one hand she rapped smartly upon the wooden door, ignoring the ornate brass knocker which hung in its center. When no answer was heard she tried the door itself and found it securely locked.

"There is but one thing left for us to do, Winchester," Miss Taphammer said upon finding the door locked, "and that is to check all other doors and windows to determine whether any means of ingress remains to us short of breaking into this house."

"Miss Taphammer!" the geographer gasped in horror, "how can you contemplate such conduct? At the least ought we not to consult with Parson Goodspeed, or consult with Mayor von der Lucans, who is probably at this moment attending to his feed and harness business?

"My heavens, what if Jeshaw Callister exits his dry goods emporium for a stroll through the town and sees us entering this house? He is still the town sheriff, you know, Miss Taphammer! Perhaps this matter had been best left to him."

"You know as well as I, Mr. Winchester Blount," said Miss Taphammer severely, "that the old fogies and their young allies who run this town have never cared for unconventional thinkers such as the Professor, still less for African persons such as the Clay man, nor at all for the offspring of the poor, however diligently they apply themselves to self-betterment, and that leaves out Herkimer.

"If this mystery is to be unraveled, it must be done by ourselves or not at all."

"Ah, Miss Taphammer, right as ever," sighed the rotund geographer, an unaccustomed melancholy replacing the usual sprightliness of his natural demeanor.

"And further," Miss Taphammer concluded, "those same backward-minded persons who are the supposed leaders of our town seek nothing but spite and revenge against any woman who dares to assert a claim to a humanity equal to that of a man. You beheld today the attitudes of Mr. Pinchard and Rev. Goodspeed. You yourself are even tainted in their regard for expressing so much as sympathy for my cause! No, no, Mr. Blount, this is a task for us alone, and if you will not offer your assistance I shall continue in solitude to pursue the disappearance of our colleague and his two companions!"

"I would not desert in a time of need," Mr. Blount replied. "Let us continue the investigation."

Miss Taphammer led the way to the rear of the Thintwhistle domicile, trying each door as it was passed, and, finding none unlocked, repeated her circuit of the edifice, trying each window as it was reached. At length one was found unlocked and, having first pushed a frame upwards a sufficient distance to admit the entry of a human form, she turned to Mr. Blount and asked him to assist her to enter.

"But, Miss Taphammer . . ." the geographer protested.

"Please, Mr. Blount," she interrupted, "do not protest so much, but merely make a step for me by lacing your fingers together that I may place my boot thereon and obtain leverage to enter the house."

"Oh my, oh my," moaned Mr. Blount, beads of perspiration dotting his fleshy brow. "Our reputations are absolutely finished if we are observed in such behavior!"

"Well then, all the more reason to be quick, so that we may get out of the prying eye of passers-by and into the sheltering concealment of the house."

"Yes, of course," murmured Mr. Blount, complying with Miss Taphammer's request and stooping to permit her to place one high-booted foot upon his hands. As he did so he averted his eyes so as not to observe the still trim ankle of the elderly but well-preserved Miss Taphammer.

In a moment he felt the weight of her person pushing downward upon his laced hands, then its removal, a scrape and a rustle from the direction of the window above, and then the voice of Miss Taphammer inviting him to follow.

He reached upward and with the assistance of a slim but surprisingly strengthful hand made his way through the window.

The room in which Miss Taphammer and Mr. Blount found themselves was a dark and comfortably furnished chamber, thick and intricately woven oriental carpets covering all except for a polished border of parquet-inlaid flooring. The furniture comprised a horsehair-stuffed settee, a number of comfortable armchairs, a reading table or desk, and a number of smoking stands. Upon the desk there stood a humidor upon opening which Miss Taphammer found it to be filled with a finely ground shag of unfamiliar hue and aroma.

The walls were lined for the most part with crowded bookshelves the contents of which reflected the interests of their owner, dealing largely with the matters of natural philosophy and dramatic declamation. The arrangement of the books had been carried out according to the dictates of some system not immediately comprehensible even to the astute mind of Miss Olivia Taphammer.

With a sweep of her lengthy skirts the lady turned from the books to the portraits which adorned those portions of wall not covered by crowded shelving. "Ah," she exclaimed, "a large daguerreotype of the Professor's Old Dad. Most touching, it is as though it were a shrine to the memory of the departed."

From a flounced taffeta cuff she drew a lady's kerchief and dabbed carefully at the corners of her eyes.

From across the room the soft voice of Mr. Winchester Blount came. "Here I note from the engraved plate at the bottom of the frame is a portrait of one Zaghlul Pasha. A most exotic-looking gentleman whom my own studies remind me is a leading jurist of the faraway nation of Egypt. How surprising to find his effigy in this house."

"Mr. Zaghlul Pasha, sir, is an associate and protégé of whom Professor Thintwhistle is most proud," Miss Taphammer informed him.

The geographer looked with widely opened eyes at his co-conspirator, but chose to make no further remark upon the subject of the foreign personage. He did, however, proceed to examine the spines of several rows of books, remarking that they must provide a sound basis for the academic qualifications of their owner.

"Indeed, and a thorough perusal of their contents, I would make so bold as to wager, would well provide us with a clew as to the mysterious disappearance and present whereabouts of the Professor and his two companions. However, I suggest that we are not possessed of sufficient leisure in which to perform the requisite examination, and would better devote ourselves to an examination of the remainder of the house in search of such clews as may be present."

So saying she proceeded to the door of the library, electing to exit by a means more conventional than that by which she had entered the room. Mr. Blount opened the mahogany door for her and Miss Taphammer stepped through, turning confidently to her right in the corridor in which she now found herself, and saying, "Let us examine the conservatoire which lies at the end of this passage."

They proceeded to do so, the geographer bursting into unrestrained expressions of rhapsody over the presence of a rare carniverous *dionaea muscipula* in the very act of devouring a large housefly which had blundered into its demesne and been so unwise as to attempt to sate its thirst upon the nectar of the flower.

A number of other vegetative marvels were exclaimed over by the rotund gentleman whose academic qualifications, while unchallenged, were based unfortunately entirely upon the study of learned works and rapt attendance upon the words of travelers and other great men, but who had, himself, traveled little and that entirely within the region of western Pennsylvania.

Never had he seen a *diococcus sloctoporus*, and only

in diagrammatic drawings the rare *lobularia maritima,* both of which grew in the rich soil and glass-protected warmth of the Professor's private garden. At length, however, he was started from a delighted revery in the presence of a flowering Asian *echinaracnius parma* by the sound of Miss Taphammer saying, "It is clear that nothing has been disturbed here nor is there present any clew as to the Professor's whereabouts.

"I propose that we treat ourselves to a light repast at the expense of Professor Thintwhistle's larder before continuing our search of the premises."

Mr. Blount again expressed amazement at the forward attitudes expressed by his female companion, but at length acceded upon wringing from her a pledge that a written stipulation would be left behind promising to reimburse the householder, if he so desired, for the value of all comestibles utilized by the intruders.

Miss Taphammer then proceeded to prepare a most exemplary gallimaufry from ingredients found in the larder of the household, the aroma of which dish brought a deep glow to the eyes of the chubby geographer and saliva to his mouth. Placing the delectable decoction in a pottery casserole in the center of the kitchen table—for, as she expressed the sentiment of the occasion, "This is not the time nor are these the circumstances for a proper or formal dinner"—Miss Taphammer signed to Mr. Blount to seat himself and tuck the provided linen napkin into his shirt collar.

She then proceeded further to scandalize the already shocked and reeling pedagogue by reciting from memory, in lieu of the customary prayer of grace to the Almighty, the famous (or infamous) address of Sojourner Truth as delivered to the Women's Rights Convention in Akron, Ohio, some thirty-three years earlier. Completing her citation of the Libyan Sibyl's ringing words with the resounding phrase, "And ain't I a woman?" Miss Taphammer again wiped a tear from her soft gray eye, tucked her handkerchief into her taffeta sleeve, spread a linen napkin upon the skirt of her dress, and said, "Pitch in."

Mr. Blount found himself rendered totally speechless by the remarkable performance of the music mistress, and was able only to concentrate upon the food before him for the remainder of the meal, this task being rendered substantially more easy and pleasant than had otherwise been the case by the fact that Miss Taphammer, in addition to her expert knowledge of the field of music and her most distressing views and conduct in the area of women's rights, was also a *chef de cuisine* unsurpassed in knowledge, taste, and resourcefulness.

So overwhelmed was Mr. Blount by the excellence of the repast served him that he burst out upon its completion, being unable to restrain himself, "Miss Taphammer, your cooking so far surpasses that of Mrs. Wander, in whose boarding house on Cedar Avenue I subsist, that I feel constrained to wonder at your continuing in the state of spinsterhood to the present late date."

For the first time that day Miss Taphammer yielded to a peal of laughter, a sound all the more startling—and pleasant—for its merry and unspoiled tone. "My dear Mr. Blount," she said, "while I am certain that the state of affairs to which you refer is one devoutly wished by most of the members of my sex, I must inform you that matrimony as we know it today results but in the oppression of one person and the supposed exaltation of another.

"Women alone in our society are denied the right to

cast the ballot, to practice in many professions, to enjoy the supposed pleasures of tobacco, to hold high public office, and in certain ways even to own, control, or dispose of property. But at least a woman alone is the mistress of her solitary domicile.

"The housewifely drudge, subject to the very command of a male individual who understands little and cares less for the pecularities of her female nature, is no better off than were the black slaves for whose freeing so terrible a war was fought a mere two decades ago, and for whose emancipation the great martyr gave his life.

"I appreciate the compliment which you intended to pay me, sir, but until such time as the roles of spouse and spouse are equalized, or at least rendered more nearly equal than they at present are, I shall carry my spinsterhood with pride."

"Hum, well, well," Mr. Blount responded, "I certainly did not intend so to, *ahem*, to arouse you, madam, to so impassioned a statement." His countenance was flushed and heated as he spoke, and there followed a protracted silence at the end of which Mr. Blount said, "May I suggest that we ignite the gas jets and resume our search."

Miss Taphammer agreed and before many minutes had passed they found themselves treading cautiously the steps which led downward to the cellar in which had been constructed the *Chester Alan Arthur*. "Ahah!" exclaimed Miss Taphammer upon espying the cradle in which the ether-flyer had been constructed and which stood now vacant and abandoned like the shell from which the chick had escaped, "See you that, my dear Winchester?"

The rotund geographer advanced to the base of the wooden framework and, laying a pudgy hand upon its curving timber, said, "It appears to be a cradle of the type used in the craft of shipbuilding."

"I agree entirely."

"But then where is the ship? There is scarce a body of water in the county which could take a craft of the size suggested by this cradle."

"Ah, Winchester, there you have the crux of the issue. As the famous Dr. Doyle has his detective state so sagely, 'Eliminate the impossible and that which remains, however unlikely it appears, must be the truth.'"

This principle the geographer was unable to refute, but failing also to grasp its implications, he spoke not at all, to the result that Miss Taphammer, at length, supplied the missing information: "If that which was built is indeed not a ship which sails some other medium than water, mayhap that medium being the universal ether?"

Mr. Blount stammered incoherently and at last seated himself, struck speechless, upon a paint-spattered workbench.

"And can we but locate Professor Thintwhistle's notebooks, now that June is upon us and the school term about to end, we will have free the time needed to duplicate the Professor's ether ship and follow him upon whatever great adventure he has already undertaken!"

CHAPTER 10
Felisia

Young Herkimer was roused from the slumberous depths of his night's restorative by the smart rapping of a slim bamboo rod across the soles of his feet; opening sleep-bleared orbs to observe the identity of his tormentor, he discovered the latter to be none other than Professor Thintwhistle who, upon observing the wakened state of his erstwhile pupil and present traveling companion, presented the lad with a beatific smile and urged him from his comfy bunk with a quick reminder of the important day which lay ahead.

In the depths of space, as the reader will surely realize if he but apply his intellectual powers for a moment's consideration, there is neither day nor night as we have become accustomed to these states of being upon the pleasant bosom of Mother Earth, but rather an unchanging condition of universal blackness punctuated by the variously colored displays of the mighty suns with which a spendthrift providence has so generously, nay profligately, populated the infinity of the heavens.

Night aboard the *Chester Alan Arthur* was an artificially induced arrangement, obtained when in the vicinity of a sun by presenting the *Arthur*'s form full a-beam to that luminary and then rotating her through a right, or ninety-degree, angle such that the base of her hull faced the source of light and heat, her very plates and boards creating the shadow in which her cabin thus lay. The ether-flyer was then anchored in such a position, assuring the duration of this artfully made night of as lengthy or as brief a period as was desired.

At the Professor's urging Herkimer rose from his bedclothes and, ducking behind a screen temporarily erected for the protection of his modesty, doffed his flannel pyjamas, bid good-day to the fuzz-clothed ducklings imprinted thereon, and proceeded with all deliberate speed to put on a fresh set of day-wear.

This task completed in the ghostly dimness of spatial night, he was assisted by Professor Thintwhistle into the modified deep-sea diving outfit which had been placed on board the *Arthur* for just such purposes, exited the flyer and hauled in the space anchor which he carefully stowed against further use should it be again needful. As he re-entered the saloon of the craft and hung his diving gear with care in its cupboard he was gratified to observe the presence in the center of the room of a fully spread *petit déjeuner*, Jefferson Jackson Clay standing smartly beside the table, while Professor Thintwhistle, cracked briar clenched in concentration between rows of glistening molars, performed those small adjustments upon the sturdy craft's controls which would rotate its hull into an attitude of bright and cheering morning light.

During the sharing of the morning repast the Professor discussed the plans for the day's activities, Jefferson being permitted to set up a small table for himself beside that of his social superiors in recognition of the day's importance and the delicacy of the maneuvers to be assayed.

The main breakfast table bore a variety of pitchers, slavers, dishes and trays, containing a modest morn-

ing's repast of sectioned grapefruit halves, toasted
muffins with marmalade and strawberry preserves,
shirred eggs, porridge with cinnamon and butter,
ham, buckwheats with blackstrap molasses, steaming
coffee for the Professor and buttered cocoa for Herkimer, and a small glass of light domestic port to top
off the dawn's nourishment.

At his smaller and plainer table Jefferson was permitted to breakfast upon a small dish of prunes, the con-
sumption of which he managed to intersperse between
the requirements of serving the meal to the others.

With dishes cleared away and cots made by the
houseman, during which activity Professor Thintwhistle and Herkimer enjoyed a morning stroll about the
saloon and the Professor beguiled away the moments
by filling Herkimer's large and jutting ears with a ra-
conteur's store of tales of his travels in the mysterious
Levant and his earliest encounters with the famed
Zaghlul Pasha, the three again assembled to receive
their day's instructions from their commander.

"Jefferson having brought our boilers to the requisite pressure," the Professor stated, "I shall shortly
throw our drive train into gear and our paddle wheels
will propel us to our intended destination, the triplex
planets Taphammer VI, VII and VIII. If conditions
appear propitious, we shall land and inquire of the native inhabitants as to the location of this solar system,
and how it may be that we find our way back either to
the lunar locale from which we were so precipitately,
a-heh, precipitated" (and here he paused for a hearty
laugh at the adroitness of his sally), "or to our home
base upon the earth, from whence we may recom-
mence our voyage with a greater care to the locale in
which we plant our flagstaff."

Having ascertained that his subordinates understood his intention to the limit of their not unbounded intellects, the Professor sent them scurrying as they had so often before to their respective duty stations while he hied himself to the Captain's Veranda and, stationing himself at the ship's master control panel, maneuvered the gear lever, let in the clutch that set the paddle wheels revolving, and spun the steering wheel in such manner as to direct the prow of the *Arthur* outward from the star Taphammer and along the plane of the ecliptic.

As the *Arthur* passed various small orbiting objects the Professor waved cheerily and called loud *halloos*, adding aside to Herkimer that while the smaller bodies were in all likelihood uninhabited, it never hurt to make an expression of friendship and goodwill, aside from which his own spirits were bubblingly good this morning *(mayhap with the aid of the domestic port,* Herkimer added mentally), and required an outlet ere he be burst asunder by them.

In due course they approached the grouping of Taphammer VI, VII and VIII, and the Professor, drawing from a case which depended from his instrument board a collapsing nautical spyglass, pointed it toward the three miniature worlds. He quickly gave vent to an expression of gratification and, calling Herkimer forward from the flyer's saloon, handed him the spyglass for a brief observation of the planets.

"A wondrous sight," Herkimer remarked, handing the glass back to its owner.

"It was not with the purpose of your aesthetic gratification that I handed you the glass," Professor Thintwhistle remarked frostily, "for all that your appreciation of the beauties of the handiwork of nature is gratifying.

"Upon those three worlds you observed, or ought to

have observed were you not distracted from so doing by a consideration of their beauty, a number of cities. Their architecture—" and at this moment the *savant* again pointed the spy-glass, as if to confirm his earlier conclusion— "is most unusual, and yet indicative of a high order of technique.

"Their arrangement is graceful and symmetrical, their construction apparently sturdy and enduring. I expect that we shall find the inhabitants of these little worlds to be a cultured race, well advanced in their understanding of nature, and in all probability well able to assist us in our quest of dear Sol."

"Ah joy!" responded Herkimer.

"Then all is forgiven, lad, and get you back as quickly as you can to your place of work." Picking up the speaking tube which depended beside the controls of the ship, he called "Jefferson, you dusky rascal, no slacking now! Keep up a full head of steam and let's to our chosen landing place!"

The *Arthur* thus sailed serenely through the starry void, proceeding away from the star Taphammer and toward the three small planets which the Professor and Herkimer had observed. The silence of the outer regions was broken only by the tranquil and comforting sounds of the ether-flyer in her untrammeled progress through the void: the low roar of her furnace, the hissing of steam in her boilers, the steady *chuf-chuf-chuf* of her cylinders working up and down in their jackets, and the *clackity-click, clackity-click* of her paddle wheels as they revolved through the universal ether, moving her rapidly and yet with a kind of scientific majesty through the starry depths.

As the *Arthur* reached her destined landing area Professor Thintwhistle reversed the paddle wheels briefly to halt her forward momentum, then setting the gear lever on *idle* he called Jefferson forward from the rear compartments where the blackamoor's diurnal tasks occurred and had him stand beside (and slightly to the rear of) Herkimer, the two of them at the foot of the stairs leading from the saloon to the Captain's Veranda.

"Look now through whatever porthole is handy, lads, and you shall see a sight unusual in the universe," he lectured, cracked briar held tight in one fist. "Beneath the hull of our plucky little craft we see a trio of small planets revolving about a common gravitational center.

"Upon all three are visible cities of similar architecture, suggestive of communication among the worlds, perhaps even of mutual visitations and commerce. This is all to the good from our point of view, for the more advanced the aborigines with whom we deal, the greater the likelihood of their being able to provide information and assistance to us.

"When we make ground, Herkimer, you will accompany me outside and join me in my efforts to communicate with the local inhabitants. You, Jefferson, will remain aboard the *Arthur* and attend to such routine duties as are appropriate during a visit which I anticipate will not be overly long."

With one hand waving a gesture of dismissal and with the other jamming his cracked and obsequious briar between his teeth, the Professor turned back to his controls and shifted the gear lever into a forward position. Sighting through the window above his instrument panel, the Professor noted that the three small planets revolved about one another rapidly and in an intricate pattern, producing at any moment a rapidly altering series of geometrical figures ranging from triangles of all possible classes to a rare linear configuration, the latter offering, when broad-on to Taphammer, an image like that of the Potawatamy County Fair's shell game, and, when end-on to the sun, a most unusual condition of eclipse.

At the moment the three planets were arranged in a semi-obtuse isosceles triangle, having emerged from an equilateral configuration and tending toward an acute. The Professor selected the planet nearest the *Arthur* by default of the three being apparently identical, and set the nose of the ether-flyer into a gentle descent aimed at the largest concentration of architecture visible upon the surface of that world.

The ether-flyer settled gently amidst a mixture of *chufs* and *clickety-clacks,* puffs of smoke and sparks from her stacks marking the site of planetfall for any who might wish to observe the event. The sturdy little ship came to rest on a grassy meadow within easy sight of the nearest buildings, which were marked by a grace of form and a blending of pastel colors most agreeable to the eye of the sensitive observer.

Leaving Jefferson within the *Arthur,* as previously planned, the Professor and Herkimer garbed themselves in raiment of the most splendid yet solemn design and coloration, in keeping with the nature of the event about to transpire, Professor Thintwhistle topping his own accoutrement with a plumed commodore's hat of midnight blue and golden frogging having but briefly flirted with the idea of wearing instead a silk topper of the Gernsback model. Herkimer polished the lid of his Callister's finest brand straw skimmer and set it firmly and squarely upon his cranium, attaching its elastic keeper to the lapel of his jacket which, as was wholly fitting, was of a more conservative cut and design than was that of his commander.

Jefferson opened the portal of the *Arthur's* saloon

and bowed the two *de facto* ambassadors through the doorway, the gravity of the moment broken only by little Cleopatra who chose to scamper and frolic about the neatly polished boots of the two plenipotentiaries and steadfastly eluded all efforts to capture her and return her to her brood, who were by now well on the way to subsisting upon a solid diet of scraps from the scullery of the ether-flyer.

Professor Thintwhistle and Herkimer set off at a brisk but dignified pace across the meadow toward the attractive town they had noted, but 'ere they had reached the edge of the grassy field Herkimer found himself sprawling suddenly with a cry of astonishment and an expression of alarm upon his physiognomy.

"What ho, lad!" his pedagogical companion exclaimed, "have you permitted the lightened gravity of this miniature globe to fool you into so clumsy a maneuver as that?"

Herkimer looked up and, upon seeing that the youth was unharmed although obviously discomfitted, "Old Tut" placed his hands upon his hips and burst into peals of jolly laughter at the sight which he beheld.

The younger man climbed to his feet, dusted himself off, replaced his skimmer and set off astride, speaking no words nor indicating the cause of his embarrassment until, with a startled *whoop* of his own, Professor Thintwhistle too went down, his splendid headpiece tumbling end for end until it came to rest in an inverted condition some several yards away.

"My word," the *savant* exclaimed, "I see now what befell you, and understand the glee with which you witness my own discomfiture. I believe that we are in the middle of a playing field set out for the game of croquet, for you see, I have caught my toe beneath a wicket and thus thrown myself to the ground, landing but lightly thanks to the reduced gravitational pull of this small world."

"Indeed, that is the very phenomenon to which I earlier fell victim," Herkimer replied, "and against which I truly ought to have given warning, save for my humiliation at your cruel laughter!"

"Revenge is yours," said Professor Thintwhistle severely, "so let us say nothing more of this matter, boy, but tread carefully lest we again find ourselves pitched down."

Thus they advanced to the end of the meadow, when, upon facing a narrow strip of paved ground before the first of the city's buildings, they noticed little Cleopatra still with them. Professor Thintwhistle whirled to look back toward the *Arthur* where Jefferson could be seen affixing the little ship's land anchor with industry, or at least as much industry as that dusky functionary was known ever to display in the sight of his employer.

Cleopatra scampered ahead of the Professor and Herkimer, and to the utter astonishment of the two travelers, as their feline pet approached closely to the first building of the local civilization, a low structure of imposing dimensions and workmanship, a horde of cats poured from the main portal, cats of every description: Persians, Siamese of every point, calicos, Burmese, alleycats, short and long-haired cats, brindles, duotones, tabbie stripes, tortoise shells, black glistening creatures with luminous green eyes, fluffy kitties, scarred veterans, children and gaffers of the cat world.

At their head strode a cat of imposing mien, white-bodied with overtones of cream, possessed of orange striped points upon all four paws, an orange striped tail with a marked crook near its tip, orange ears and

mask, and blue eyes of a brilliance of hue combined
with a mildness of expression to capture the very heart
of any fancier of *felis catus* in any of his variform
manifestations.

Imagine the incredulity of the Professor and "Herk"
when this magnificent example of catdom, after pausing to stroke his fine whiskers authoritatively, addressed himself to little Cleopatra and in a clearly
ringing baritone voice said "Madame, in behalf of the
City of Catterstall I bid you welcome and invite you
to enter our borders."

Cleopatra, of course, ignored these words save for a
puzzled jerk of her head, and proceeded to attack a
stray boot-lace depending from the polished footwear
of Herkimer.

The large cream-and-orange Tom paused briefly, as
if for an answer which was naturally not forthcoming,
then repeated his statement verbatim, although in an
even more ringing tone than previously. Still there was
no response from Cleo, whereupon the many cats in
the entourage of the speaker, who had until this moment maintained a perfect silence among themselves,
fell to whispering and buzzing busily to one another,
precisely as might a crowd of courtiers in the presence
of an earthly monarch!

"Remarkable!" exclaimed Professor Thintwhistle to
Herkimer. "Had I not heard with my own ears, I had
discounted as purest fabrication any report to reach
me of a talking cat, the which we seem to find ourselves confronting this very moment!"

Before the dumbfounded Herkimer had gathered
sufficient of his wits and his voice to make any intelligible reply to this statement, astonishment was piled
upon amazement as the cat spokesman turned toward
the two humans for the first time and said "Am I de-

ceived, or did I hear feline speech emerging from the lips of these two clumsy and gigantic beings?"

At once the army of cats fell again to discussion of what must, to them, appear a marvel of near miraculous proportion, while Professor Thintwhistle and the now-recovered Herkimer proceeded similarly to make note of the wonder of these denizens of the cat kingdom apparently given over not merely to intelligent thought (of which any cat fanicer is aware that all cats are capable in any case) but to human-sounding speech.

Gathering about him all of his aplomb which remained unimpaired by the strange situation in which he found himself, Professor Thintwhistle advanced to a position facing the cat monarch and, lowering himself to one knee in order more easily to converse with the wonderful creature (an act which the latter interpreted as a gesture of respect, a natural misunderstanding but one which would shortly redound to the advantage of the two earthly travelers) gave voice as follows: "Sir Cat, unless I am mistaken, you have just spoken intelligibly, in well-formed and chosen words, the first member of your tribe ever, to my knowledge, to do so."

"Sir Giant," the cat responded, "our own astonishment at this event is no less than your own, for we had until this time believed that all cats, and only cats, were gifted by their maker with this ability, whereupon in the small space of a few moments we encounter first a cat," and he indicated little Cleo, "incapable of speech, whom we had considered for the moment the victim of a mental deficiency, and now the spectacle of you, Sir Giant, a creature of a breed and dimension never before encountered in the combined histories of the three worlds of Felisia, aleph, beth and gimmel, capable not only of the formation of intelligible words but also, apparently, of cat-like thought and understanding!"

'What!" exclaimed the *savant*. "You mean that you are not merely capable of speech, but that your tribe has developed this talent untutored by human agency?"

"Such indeed is the case, Sir Giant. We may add, further, our astonishment at the fact that you are not merely capable of speech, but that the tongue which you utilize is the Felisian."

"The Felisian," rejoined the Professor in surprise. "But, Sir Cat, the language I speak is the English language, the speech of the most advanced race of men upon the planet of my origin. How come you to speak it, and to call it by the name Felisian rather than English?"

This anomaly caused several moments of consternation upon both sides in the strange dialogue, which impasse was broken by the words of a large Manx in the entourage of the cat monarch, a magnificent tailless tom of perfect orange-striped and purest white configuration, who strode to the fore of the cat party and, in gruff but authoritative manner proclaimed the following: "My liege lord, and Sir Giant, were you but familiar with the theories of the great feline philosopher Lady Mehitabel, you had heard of the theory of infinite creation.

"The Lady Mehitabel, in her remarkable work on metaphysics, posits a universe endless in scope and eternal in duration, in which, logic requires, all possible configurations of essence, *however farfetched*, providing only that they do not directly violate the laws of nature, must needs find embodiment in reality at some point of time or space.

"Thus the parallel development of identical languages on different and wholly separate worlds, since it is possible, albeit of a very low order of probability, must needs occur. Such a case we have today encountered, and, while highly remarkable and in all probability of historic note, this occurrence, by simple virtue of being possible under the laws of the universe, was inevitable."

With these remarkable words the assertive Manx resumed his place in the entourage of the cat monarch, leaving the latter, and Professor Thintwhistle, equally impressed and dumbfounded at the brilliance of the Manx's citation and its obvious applicability to the present unprecedented state of affairs.

CHAPTER 11
The Transfer

Throughout the amazing converse which took place among Professor Thintwhistle and the two leading representatives of Felisia's feline folk, young Herkimer had stood watching and listening, his attention held by the unusual aspect of the occurrence of rational discourse between humanity and animalkind, but as the conversation wore on, and especially as the gruff-mannered Manx persisted in declaiming the philosophy of the great feline metaphysician Mehitabel, "Herk" found his attention wandering farther and farther from the conversation at hand.

At first he inspected the army of cats headed by the cream-and-orange monarch and the harsh-voiced Manx, comparing them with the appearance and conduct of little Cleo who frolicked and pounced about the feet of the humans, then he shifted his gaze upwards to the city of the Felisians rising above and standing behind the corps of cats, gay banners waving from sturdily constructed buildings and broad boulevards running hither and yon among them.

Of particular note, and to Herkimer's inquiring mind of signal interest, was the presence on the sidewalks, in ranks upon the boulevards, and even upon the walls and ledges of buildings, of a very massive number of croquet wickets.

Even this oddity palled in time, and as the scholarly discourse continued Herkimer clasped his well-manicured hands in the small of his back and, tilting his head back, gazed upward into the sky of the planet Felisia upon which he stood, and was astonished at being able to perceive, even in the daylight provided by the star Taphammer (the local name of which he did not know), the other two members of the Felisian planet group. They stood in the sky, which was itself of a remarkable hue and pattern, one near the horizon and ascending rapidly, the other halfway to the zenith and approaching it as well from a direction some ninety degrees away from the first.

At precisely this moment there was heard radiating from the buildings of the cat city a sound unprecedented in the experience of the lad, as though the sound of a multiplicity of guitar strings were being plucked simultaneously and amplified through a gigantic megaphone. The loud sound produced a ringing in Herkimer's ears which persisted for many moments after the termination of the sound, by which time Professor Thintwhistle could be heard inquiring of the cat monarch as to the source and meaning of the phenomenon which had just transpired.

"Ah, Sir Giant, there is no cause for alarm; in fact you are most fortunate in the timing of your visit to the Felisian group, for the sound which was just heard was the first warning to unwary citizens of the imminent approach of a Transfer. There remains sufficient time to accomplish such tasks as may be needful before the Transfer occurs, and you may of course choose freely as to whether you wish to participate or to remain upon Felisia aleph, although, in view of the rarity of the occurrence of Transfers, I should expect you to elect participation."

"Transfer, Sir Cat?" inquired the Professor, who had by now exchanged his former kneeling position for a more comfortable and easily maintained yogic posture, no doubt learned from some of his exotic and Bohemian associates of past years. "Pray, what is the meaning of a Transfer?"

"Ah," the cat monarch responded, settling himself as well into a position of comfort and pausing to scratch a possible flea from behind one royal ear with a royal hind paw, "this is a matter of physical science and I will call once again upon Sir Purrfurr, our court adviser most versed in such matters, to provide you with a correct explanation of the phenomenon."

So saying he waved his royal paw in the direction of the gruff-mannered Manx who again advanced to participate in the parley, his grumpy exterior ill-concealing the pleasure which he felt at being asked for elucidation of the mysterious Transfer.

Sir Purrfurr bowed to his monarch, nodded sagely to Professor Thintwhistle, and, seating himself upon the sward between them pointed sagely at the very celestial phenomena which had recently captured the attention of Herkimer. "As you are aware, Sir Giant," the Manx said, "Felisia comprises not one but three small planets, all revolving about one another or, more accurately, about a common center. The orbits of the three Felisian planets, which we choose to call Felisia aleph, Felisia beth, and Felisia gimmel—you are presently seated upon the soil of Felisia aleph—manifest complex relationships which are reflected in the continually altering spatial relationships of the three planets themselves.

"Each planet possesses a gravitic field of its own, the fields of the others having but little effect except in the matter of raising tides, save for the rare occasion of positioning of the three planets in direct alignment with one another. When this transpires, all cats and other loose objects upon the far side of each outer planet are drawn down to their world with not merely the normal attraction of their own planet, but with the attraction of both other planets as well, pulling coaxially with that of the said outer planet.

"Those situated upon the face of the end planets directed toward the center planet, however, find themselves simultaneously drawn downward by the gravitic attraction of their own planet only, but drawn straight upward by the simultaneous attraction of the other *two* planets. As you will immediately perceive, the upward pull of two gravities exceeds in force the downward pull of but one, and we are drawn into the air, flying on nature's own wings through the atmosphere and in fact with great chunks of it which also fly, to land safely and comfortably at the end of a most thrilling journey, upon the face of the center planet.

"In this manner the three planets of Felisia periodically shift populations from one to another, assuring the cultural continuity of the great people of the Felisian system."

Professor Thintwhistle found himself highly impressed with the clarity of Sir Purrfurr's logic, expressing himself to this end when the latter had completed his peroration, for, in fact, the pedagogue felt himself already growing appreciably lightheaded as the two other planets of the grouping, Felisia beth and gimmel, approached the point of alignment directly overhead.

"But what," Professor Thintwhistle asked, "of such citizens as would prefer to remain upon the planet of their present residence?"

"The answer to that is simple," interrupted the cat

monarch. "As you may have noticed, earlier generations of Felisians have placed many metallic loops in
the ground, streets, and buildings of our city, Catterstall, and any citizen caught out-of-doors at the moment of Transfer need merely grasp such an one securely and wait for the continued progress of beth and
gimmel to disalign the planets, ending the Transfer,
upon which development the citizen's feet drop once
more to the ground and he is able to pursue his usual
round of business; although, naturally, he will find
many of his friends and associates absent until a Transfer occurs during which aleph is the central of the
three planets."

At this moment a loud note as of an organ chord
was heard coming from Catterstall, which the king explained as the second warning call of the forthcoming
Transfer.

"Such radical and massive relocations of population
must cause great dislocations in the commercial and
personal intercourse among Felisian citizens," Professor Thintwhistle commented.

"Indeed so," responded his majesty, "but they are
nonetheless looked forward to with great relish by
some citizens, and provide a salutary lesson for all, in
view of our custom of canceling all contractual relationships among citizens participating in a Transfer."

"All, Sir Cat?"

"Indeed all, Sir Giant! Debts and obligations are
canceled, all property is abandoned, marriages are dis-
solved, wealth is left behind to be divided among
newcomers to the Transferred vicinity, children are
freed of the authority of their parents and parents of
the responsibility for their children, governments
cease to hold power, and all citizens begin anew upon
an equal footing."

"Such a system possesses obvious merit," said Professor Thintwhistle, "but has it not also within it the seeds of brutal injustice?"

"Perhaps," shrugged the cat, "but our experience is that infants are adopted and cared for, new governments are formed, commerce resumes and the general life of society is preserved—but with a freshness and verve associated with new undertakings. Further, the clever or greedy are prevented from amassing too great or too enduring fortunes, while the poor and the distressed are enabled to start anew with old debilities wiped out."

"And is there no commerce between worlds except at moments of Transfer?" the Professor inquired.

"We do maintain a few small craft for interplanetary travel in case of emergency, but they are neither numerous nor frequently utilized."

At this moment a sound was heard as of a great gong being struck, and Professor Thintwhistle felt himself growing lighter and lighter until he was utterly weightless and began to float gently into the Felisian sky. Looking upward he observed the planets Felisia beth and Felisia gimmel sliding into an attitude of perfect alignment.

It was the moment of Transfer, and Professor Thintwhistle, Cleo, Herkimer, the cat monarch, Sir Purrfurr, and the entire feline corps were drifting gently into the air.

For a moment the Professor instinctively clutched at a staple projecting from the Felisian ground, then felt his prized commodore's hat of dark blue and gold frogging detach itself from his grizzled locks and proceed upon its journey without him. Casting caution to the winds, the Professor called "Come along, Herkimer!", relaxed his grasp upon the staple, snatched successfully with his other hand for his commodore's hat and, resettling it firmly upon his well-filled cranium, began to dig cheerfully into a capacious pocket for the cracked and Parnassian briar with which we have all become so familiar.

As the great body of individuals rose gently into the air above the city of Catterstall, Professor Thintwhistle permitted his own gaze to travel about him, remarking to himself upon the unprecedented sight of himself and his protégé Herkimer flying upward, Herkimer tumbling comically with arms and legs akimbo, the *savant* serenely puffing his briar while maintaining a comfortable yogic posture with legs crossed and spine erect, the two of them quite surrounded by an army, a tribe, a fleet, a virtual nation of cats, cats above, cats beneath, cats to all sides, tumbling, meowing, chatting amiably, remarking upon the beauty of the day and the smoothness of the Transfer.

Professor Thintwhistle took this opportunity to reach into an inner pocket of his splendid coat and draw therefrom a miniature replica of the folding spyglass he had used to observe celestial features from the cabin of the *Chester Alan Arthur* and, extending the small optical instrument to its full length, the pedagogue, still maintaining his yogic cross-legged posture, instituted a paddling movement with one hand, altering his position relative to the air flow in which he and his companions, both human and feline, moved.

In this manner the Professor caused his own body to rotate like a miniature planet, facing first this way, then that, toward Felisia aleph, then toward Felisia beth and gimmel beyond, in between examining in greater detail than ever the objects and features of the Taphammer system and surrounding celestial landmarks.

Upon one such rotation he recognized Cleo, who, having initially responded to her surprising aerial locomotion with alarm, had become accustomed to her movement and gave every indication of enjoying the sensation of weightlessness and the delight of swooping this way and that with each errant air current while she rose through the atmosphere—or, more precisely, *with* much of the atmosphere—of Felisia aleph. At this moment she had stretched her little limbs to their uttermost extent and showed her tiny needle-like teeth in a yawn that was, for one so small as she, a virtual abyss. Professor Thintwhistle propelled himself to her side and, guiding her silky form to a comfortable position upon his lap, was gratified to observe her curling up into an attitude of confident repose, whereupon she closed her yellow eyes and began to purr loudly.

Noting that the disk of Felisia aleph had shrunk and that of beth had grown to that point at which they were of equal size in the heavens, Professor Thintwhistle spied out his friend the feline monarch from among the horde of furry Felisians surrounding him and made ready to address him concerning this state of affairs.

"Sir Cat," the Professor began, but the words had no more than passed from his lips than the feline interrupted, albeit gently and with an utter absence of ire.

"Sir Cat for the moment, Sir Giant," said the cream and orange Felisian, "but shortly to be merely Albert Arthur William Frederick George Michael Farquar von Hohenzollern Smythe, gentlecat, for as you may have noted we are already at the halfway point in our journey and as soon as we reach Felisia beth I shall be king no longer, but an ordinary subject in the court of King Clement VII of Felisia beth."

"You may call me Al."

The Professor expressed his gratitude at the implied familiarity permitted by the monarch, however short might be the remaining portion of his reign, continuing to inquire as to the likely manner of their landing upon and reception in Felisia beth.

"We shall land as gently as we rose," the cat monarch responded, "for as we approach the surface of Felisia beth we shall be slowed by a compacting column of air being pushed ahead of and pressed beneath our bodies.

"As for the reception which we will receive, it is the inviolable custom of our people that individuals arriving at the end of a Transfer are greeted as honored guests, welcomed with a great festival which dates to the time long ago when the Transfer was not understood and was believed to be a miracle. For three days and three nights we shall be feted, carried in splendor through the streets of Fritzburg, the chief city of Felisia beth.

"We shall travel the world and meet new arrivals from Felisia gimmel which, you will recall, is presently situated upon the opposite side of Felisia beth. Perhaps I shall again" (and a tear seemed for a moment to glisten in the eye of the cream-and-orange) "see my litter mates, from whom I have been separated since the last Transfer.

"At the end of the festival we shall all be left to our own devices, but it is the further custom of Felisia that new arrivals are offered the hospitality of Felisian homes, fed, cared for, and provided with employment commensurate with their abilities." The cat floated gracefully in the air for a few moments, when from behind him there was heard a gruff voice.

Both "Al" and the Professor turned to see Sir Purrfurr, the monarch's adviser, floating toward them through the air. Being a Manx he lacked the sinuous and graceful feline tail which permitted Albert and the others of the Felisian race to balance themselves in the air, but for the lacking caudal appendage he substituted a sure and precise sense of balance which permitted him to duplicate the maneuvers of even the most generously endowed cat.

"What plans have you, Sir Giant?" asked the Manx.

"That is a story of considerable length and complexity," the Professor replied, "but in the time remaining to us before our arrival at Fritzburg I shall attempt to provide you with a capsulized version."

So saying the Professor launched himself upon a brief narrative description of the voyage of the *Chester Alan Arthur* from the moment of its launching from Revolutionary Hill to the present moment, at the end of which narration he indicated the still helplessly spinning Herkimer, who had gone into an orbit with his straw skimmer, and said, "We shall have to arrange for our manservant, Jefferson, to bring the *Arthur* across the space separating Felisia aleph from beth, so that we may be reunited and continue our search for home. We should hope first to obtain an audience with a conclave of Felisia's most learned *savants* in order to obtain a clew as to our whereabouts with relationship to our parent sun."

"You are already addressing Felisia's most learned *savant*," the Manx pronounced gravely. "Modesty might cause me to hesitate so to inform you, Sir Giant, but honesty requires that I do so nonetheless. The struggle of the two has troubled me often, but honesty inevitably emerges triumphant."

"I have been faced with a similar difficulty in my own home," the pedagogue responded, "and with the same inevitable outcome."

"Well, then," said the Manx, permitting his voice to trail off into silence.

"Still, rather than consult a single cat, I should hope to address a convocation of experts in all the natural philosophies. Might this not be arranged, under the chairmanship of a suitable individual such as yourself?"

"Ah, well, now that you make that suggestion I suppose that such a conference might well prove to be of educational value to many of my less advanced colleagues, and at the same time productive of assistance to yourself."

At this moment the Professor turned his eyes groundward and found that while he and his hosts had conversed, they had approached closely to Felisia beth and were about to make their landing.

Herkimer was seen to tumble to the ground, nearly duplicating the crash of so far away which had precipitated him outside the gate of Professor Thintwhistle in Buffalo Falls. The lad picked himself up, replaced his straw skimmer which was by this juncture beginning to look somewhat the worse for wear, and dusted himself off. He was promptly surrounded by a crowd of curious Felisians who had stood waiting the arrival of the travelers from aleph.

Professor Thintwhistle landed so gently that he remained seated with his legs crossed and little Cleo sound asleep upon his lap. Al and Purrfurr alighted nearby, the former commenting upon the surprising grace of the Professor's first landing.

"Old Tut," still holding his small spyglass, turned it upon the surface of the planet they had but recently quitted and, after squinting through the instrument for a moment dropped the glass with a curse and

smacked the fist of one hand into the palm of the
other, a beet-red hue creeping from his collar to his
noble brow.

"We are betrayed, darling boy!" the *savant* cried to
Herkimer, the years of care and labor which he had so
long and strongly borne making themselves for the
first time visible upon his venerable countenance.

The innocent-visaged lad said, "What can you
mean, dear mentor?"

"I mean that rascally blackamoor," the Professor exploded. "I mean that treacherous son of Ethiop!"

"Yes, sir," responded Herkimer, "but what is it that
Jefferson has done, so to provoke your outrage?"

"That worthless scamp," ejaculated Professor Thintwhistle, pointing angrily skyward with the stump of
his briar, which he had finally, in his moment of su-
preme rage, bitten through, "that ungrateful baboon
has absconded with our ether-flyer!"

He passed the spyglass to Herkimer who, after first
placing it wrong-end-to against his eye, accidentally
folded it in the process of attempting to correct his
error, then unfolded it and at length succeeded in training it properly upon that portion of the sky from which
the marvelous Transfer had brought them.

High above them in the sunny dome of Felisia beth
he could see a tiny image moving away from the mottled disk of Felisia aleph. From it there trailed a series
of still tinier dots of black smoke, which slowly faded
into the interplanetary blackness. In his mind's ear
Herkimer could even hear the homey *chuf-chuf-chuf-*
and *clickety-clack* of the ether-flyer's propulsive mechanisms.

"What can he be doing?" inquired Herkimer of the
Professor, a tremor in his voice.

When there was no immediate response from the

apoplectic pedagogue, Herkimer assayed an optimistic guess. "Perhaps he has decided to follow us without our having sent for him."

To this the Professor responded by pointing again scornfully in the direction of the tiny planet which swam overhead. Beside it could be seen the small silhouette of the *Chester Alan Arthur* as the sturdy ship piloted by Jefferson and carrying Cleopatra's now virtually orphaned offspring, grew smaller, smaller yet, and at length disappeared into the distant darkness.

Professor Thintwhistle turned at the feel of a sympathetic paw upon his shoulder and, looking into the kindly face of ex-king Al, said, "It is good to know in times such as this that one is not without friends."

CHAPTER 12
The Crispus Attucks

From the Cabin Boy's Log, Ether Date 1884.0802:

First of all, as the sole human being remaining aboard the ether-flyer I am assuming the captaincy at once and as my first official act as captain renaming the *Chester Alan Arthur,* which will be known henceforth as the *Crispus Attucks.*

Secondly, in keeping with my new position and as symbol of my revolutionary break with the oppression of the past I am abandoning my former name of Jefferson Jackson Clay and rechristening myself Menelik XX Chaka, by which name I will henceforth be known.

Having successfully ditched the ofays T and H, I am now proceeding away from the star system Taphammer and will attempt rendezvous with Captain L y A and his progressive forces, thereafter to develop such plans as are appropriate for the furthering and inevitable victory of our sacred Movement. More anon.

Venceremos!

Chaka, Captain

With a sureness and skill born of long if clandestine familiarity with the most complex of the ether-

flyer's mechanisms, Captain Chaka locked the craft
into a parking orbit two-and-one-half parsecs out from
Taphammer. He equipped himself with paintpot,
brush, astrolabe and compass, donned the captain's
vacuum suit and exited from the cabin of the ship.

Outside in the blackness of intra-Selenate space he
attached a tether to his belt, fixed the other end smartly to a dogging ring on the exterior of the craft, and
proceeded about his business, the first order of which
was the careful obliteration of the old name of the
ether craft and its replacement with the revolutionary
name *Crispus Attucks.*

This task completed and the paintpot re-covered so
that stray droplets of pigment would not be scattered,
Chaka proceeded to sight upon the now-distant star
Taphammer, correlating in his mind the position of
the star, that of the *Attucks,* the orbit in which the
ship was now parked and the path upon which she
had approached Taphammer. With a grunt of satisfaction he hauled upon his tether, re-entered the cabin of
the craft and doffed his space garb.

Humming a revolutionary tune he proceeded to the
roll-top desk in the rear of the craft, pulled a hortatory
poster from one of its many concealed pigeon-holes
and affixed it to the ship's bulkhead above the instrument panel on the Captain's Veranda. Chaka undogged the controls of the ship, made a quick notation
upon a star-chart which was set up beside the control
panel, and set the ether-flyer in motion upon a course
that carried it steadily away from the star Taphammer
and in a direction plotted by him.

The ship's furnace roared with a high and steady
flame, the boiler hissed and bubbled powerfully, the
cylinders moved up and down in their jackets with a
steady *chuf-chuf-chuf* and the paddle wheels, upon

the application of a drop of oil to a strategic shaft, substituted a steady burring sound for their former *clickety-clacking*.

Captain Chaka locked the controls in place, pulled the ship's folding spyglass from its case and retired to a porthole from which to survey the splendors of the star-bedecked heavens. As he swept the varicolored suns and comets of the void with his spyglass he hummed militantly to himself, "Revolutionary peoples of the emerging world, overtake British industrial indices by 1901."

Far in the distance of the strange intra-Selenate space the *Escarabajo de Plata* sailed on, her sheets bellied full with an ether wind unknown upon the seas of earth, her captain sitting troubled in his own lantern-lighted cabin, the former Jefferson Jackson Clay's note clutched in his Spanish hand, its words running over and over through Captain Lupe y Alvarado's mind as his keen, dark eyes passed again and again over the scrawled words on the piece of ship's-stores flimsy before him.

Himself a Levantine citizen by birth, he had become convinced that popular theories as to the shape of the earth were false and had travelled the Mediterranean world in search of a man of wealth and power who would finance an expedition westward across the Atlantic in search of a new route to the spices and silks of the Indies which would replace the lengthy and expensive caravan routes which traders had used from time immemorial.

The merchants and princes of Greece, the traders and consuls of neo-Republican Rome, the People's Revolutionary Council of the Holy Mithraic Frankish See had all listened courteously to his theories, dismissed him as a typical Hebrew fanatic, and had sent him on his way with polite encouragement but no tangible backing.

Ironically it was in Iberia, the land of his ancestors' birth and the source of his own purebred ethnic heritage, that the Tsar and Tsarina, motivated clearly by the hope of a trading coup rather than by any thirst for the expansion of human knowledge, had outfitted for him a small fleet of three many-sailed galleons, provided crews dragged up from the waterside warrens of the nation's ports, and set him, Juan Diego Salvador José Domingo de Lupe y Alvarado at their head as captain, to act in the names of Isidro y Fernanda.

And now, having sailed over the edge of the world into apparent disaster, and having survived the fall to the total astonishment of all concerned and set sail upon a new etheric sea, he and his officers and crew had encountered that incredible closed craft, the *Arthur*. With what startlement had Captain Lupe y Alvarado heard the tale of the *Arthur*'s captain, and with what astonishment had he read the message surreptitiously delivered to him by the *Arthur*'s lowly cabin boy!

Again his eyes swept the crinkled sheet:

> *Revolutionary peoples of all planets unite! Strike down the running dogs of oppression, capitalism, colonialism and the hollow earth movement! Crush left-wing deviationism! Resist right-wing revisionism! Overcome polycentrist divisionism!*
> *Meet me after school behind the grandstands!*

The note was signed, simply, *A Friend*.

Captain Lupe y Alvarado scratched his head, wondering what the enigmatic message could mean. Captain Thintwhistle, he felt, must most assuredly be a madman, but the cabin boy was another matter. Apparently astute far beyond the expectations of his humble office, he had slipped the message into Lupe's sombrero as the latter was in the very act of leaving the *Arthur* but had given no overt clue as to his intentions.

What could it signify?

The captain refolded the flimsy note and shoved it into a fold in his voluminous britches, then rose, went to the door of his cabin, called to a nearby sailor and ordered him to summon the executive officer for a conference.

In short order there was a knock on the captain's door. "Come," he said.

The door opened and a small, swarthy fellow entered, suspicious eyes darting this way and that. He looked about the captain's cabin, then back into the passageway behind him. He closed the door carefully and slid into a wooden chair proffered by Lupe.

"Mister Limon," the captain said, "or Pablo if you do not mind informality, I think it time for us to have a serious talk about the progress of this voyage."

"Yes, sir," the small man replied, pointed nose and black moustache twitching like the nose and whiskers of a nervous rat. "I agree that it would be well to consider our situation."

"Pablo, what is the status of the ship, and what is the state of mind of the crew? We were close to mutiny before we fell off the edge of the world. Where are we now?"

"The ship is in good condition, Captain. Our supplies of food are not great but are steadily replenished so that our reserves of hardtack and jerky are almost untouched and the bins of sea biscuit are nearly full. Water is plentiful, especially since the great storm of a few days past.

"But the men are not in such good spirits. Their regard for the officers rose greatly when we brought them safely through the great fall, but they now fear that we are forever lost and will sail without aim or end through this great black sea."

The captain rubbed his chin reflectively. Without speaking he walked to a cupboard and returned to the table at which he and Mister Limon had sat, placing upon it a bottle of dry oporto and two glasses. "Well, Pablo," he said finally, "let us have a small glass to refresh ourselves before we speak more."

The *Escarabajo de Plata's* rigging creaked and the ship shifted suddenly as a gust in the invisible ether wind shook the galleon; the executive officer's shifty eyes snapped to the captain's porthole as this happened, and Captain Lupe took advantage of the momentary inattention of his executive officer to slip a small amount of fine powder into one of the two goblets.

"Here now," he said, pouring a healthy portion of oporto into each glass. He concentrated his gaze upon the bottle as he restoppered it with its porous Portuguese cork, Mister Limon taking this opportunity to slip a small amount of fine powder into one of the two goblets.

The captain said, "Would you be so good as to look under my bunk, Pablo, and bring me the large chart of the world you will find there." As the smaller man moved to obey the captain used this opportunity to arrange the goblets carefully upon the table between them.

"My apologies, Captain," Mister Limon said from

his position bending beside the bunk, "but I cannot find the chart here."

The captain moved across the cabin, Mister Limon deferentially stepping aside to give his commander access to the narrow space beneath the bunk, where the ship's charts were stored. As the captain squatted to search, Mister Limon used the opportunity to return to the table and rearrange the goblets in such manner that they appeared unmoved but were in fact in positions opposite to those in which the captain had placed them.

The captain turned and rose, a parchment roll in one hand, and returned to stand beside the table, carefully spreading the parchment upon it so that Mister Limon was forced to remove goblets and bottle and replace them upon a sideboard which stood nearby.

"Now, Pablo, a toast to their majesties Isidro and Fernanda." He lifted his goblet, staring sinisterly at his subordinate as the latter did the same.

Captain and executive tilted their heads backward and quaffed their goblets of oporto with ostentious exhibitions of enjoyment. "Ah, now that is done," they exclaimed simultaneously, bursting into good-natured but portentous laughter at the coincidence.

"Can you, Pablo, locate for me our position upon the chart before us," the captain requested solemnly.

Smiling a secret smile the meaning of which was concealed from his commanding officer, Mister Limon bent over the chart, tracing with a thin and black-nailed finger a line from the hand-drawn great falls which marked the *Escarabajo*'s entry into the etheric sea, past shoals and storms, markings of the many events which had transpired since their removal from the blue Atlantic, passing most recently a small sketch which indicated their encounter with the *Chester Alan*

Arthur, and terminating at their present position far between any two stars or other features recognizable upon the chart.

"We are here, sir," he said in his usual oleaginous manner.

"Very good, Pablo," replied Captain Lupe y Alvarado in his own customary cultured tones. "Do you see any hope of our finding our way home from here?"

For a moment before he replied, Mister Limon suffered an instant of blurred vision and a weakness passed through his thin limbs. But he clutched the edge of the table and replied, in a voice carefully steadied as he spoke, "Captain, I believe that we are hopelessly lost."

Captain Lupe y Alvarado made to speak further to Limon, but for the most brief interval he heard a loud ringing in his ears and thought that firebombs were exploding in his eyeballs. Cold perspiration broke upon his swarthy brow and a tremor passed through his body.

Regaining control of himself he lowered himself carefully into his chair and spoke with great care. "Very well, Pablo, what recommendation have you to make?"

Mister Limon felt his knees grow watery and the palms of his hands become clammy even as the captain spoke to him. With an effort he lowered himself into his own chair and said, "Captain, this is a matter of gravest import. May I suggest a further tot of oporto before giving you my recommendation?"

The captain heard Limon's words as from afar. Feeling cold, remote, he managed with great deliberation to cause himself to nod assent.

The executive officer reached carefully for the bottle of oporto, controlling the tremors of his clammy hands as he did so. He unstoppered the bottle and, struggling to keep from giving way to the ague which tried to shake his entire scrawny frame, poured two sloppy goblets full of the red wine.

The captain reached forward through a strange mist, buzzings and ringings filling his head, his throat tight, an icy flame roaring in his belly, and grasped the goblet nearer to Mister Limon by its heavy neck. "Shalom aleichem!" he managed to gasp, lifting the goblet with trembling fingers to down its contents.

"Aleichem shalom!" Limon responded, forcing the words from between puffed lips and yellow teeth clenched in a paralysis which slowly spread through his body. He managed to swallow a strangely bitter mouthful of the oporto before the remainder dribbled down his chin and onto a greasy and ill-kept doublet.

Captain Lupe slumped forward, his face lying upon the parchment chart that covered the table, his glazing eyes locked with those of his swarthy executive officer. "I want you to know, Pablo," he was able to whisper, "that your treachery has been long known to me. That you had betrayed our monarchs the Tsar and Tsarina and were in the pay of the Moorish Emperor at Tangier. And so I have . . . I have . . ." At this point the commander's voice failed him and he lay unmoving, barely breathing with his head upon the chart table.

"And you," Pablo Limon hissed between convulsively clenched teeth, "you double traitor, betraying the Levant to sail for Spain and Spain to work secretly for the Holy Mithraic Frankish See. I spit on you!" And the executive officer attempted to live up to his words, but from his puffed lips came only a feeble exhalation of fetid breath.

From the companionway outside Captain Lupe y

Alvarado's cabin there came to the fast-fading consciousness of the two officers the sound of approaching footsteps. There was a moment of silence as ears were pressed against the wood of the door, then the door swung open on its unoiled hinges and a pushing, disorderly crowd of ill-washed and ill-spoken sailors shouldered their way through the doorway and into the—by their crude standards—palatial luxury of the captain's cabin.

In the lead was a brawny fellow missing one eye and one hand, the former replaced by a black patch held in place by a filthy ribbon tied about his head; the latter, by a wickedly pointed hook which he kept assiduously polished and honed to a needle-like tip. He swaggered rather than walked, and as he reached the chart table upon which lay the two nearly unconscious officers the eyes of both Limon and Lupe y Alvarado could be seen to stare dully at him.

"Argh, so the two wretches have done each other in," the sailor roared. He lifted the heads of both by the hair and stared into both their faces. "Throw 'em to the sharks, boys, they're as good as done for already!" he snarled.

A handful of sailors advanced to drag the unmoving forms of the captain and his executive from the room, one sailor daring to mention that in these strange "waters" there was no sign of sharks.

Like lightning the hook of the other flashed out, catching the speaker by the front of his shirt. "When *El Raton Miguelito* speaks, you hop, scurvy scum! No answers back on this ship from now on. I am the captain now, does anyone dispute that?"

With his one eye he glared angrily about the cabin, taking into his blood-lustful glance the faces of all those who gathered around the chart table.

No one spoke. At length El Raton Miguelito snarled, "Then get about doing what you've been told, and watch out lest you follow this carrion into the sea!"

The sailors dragged the unmoving forms of Captain Lupe y Alvarado and Mister Limon from the cabin, others who had crowded around the doorway making room for them as they passed. After the last of the party had left, El Raton Miguelito sprawled greedily on the captain's bunk, contemplating the woodwork of the beams above it. He lay thus, thinking for a few moments, then strode to the door and shouted for a fellow sailor, one known as The Skull in recognition of the shrunken look of his face and head and his flesh-less, bony body, to join him in the captain's quarters.

As The Skull entered El Raton motioned him to the chair not long vacated by the body of Mister Limon, heaving his own greater bunk into the more comfort-able seat previously occupied by the former captain. "Skull," snarled the new captain, "now that I have taken command of the *Escarabajo* I will have need of officers I can trust. During our days together in the fo'c'stle I found you a man who could keep his ears and eyes open and his mouth shut. That's the kind I want around me.

"How would you like to be my first officer?"

The Skull grinned sardonically. "What's in it for me?"

El Raton threw back his head and roared with laughter. "What's in it for you? Ah, ye greedy scut, I should have known better than to trifle with a man who looks like a death's head.

"Well, here's what's in it for you. I propose to haul down the Tsarist pennon from the mast of the *Escara-bajo* and hoist the Jolly Roger in its place. That should please you, Skull—it looks enough like you to be a bony portrait.

"Then we'll sweep these inner seas of all the loot they can bear and share it out with the boys, share and share alike, no favorites and no privileges."

He paused significantly, then, seeing that The Skull was prepared more to listen than to talk, El Raton added, "Of course there'll be a little private session before the shares are divided, and a few of the glitteriest prizes won't be seen when sharing time comes. Now, what do you think of my offer in view of that?"

The Skull stared into the face of El Raton and said, "I don't suppose you'd want me back in the fo'c'sle knowing what you've just told me, so it's take the offer or feed the fishes, ain't it, Cap'n?"

El Raton chuckled evilly and said, "So it is, Skull."

"Well then, I suppose you've got yourself a first officer, Raton!" And so saying The Skull reached across the table with a filth-encrusted paw and seized the new captain's glistening hook in it. The two new officers shook heartily, sealing their new bargain of crime, then fell to studying the chart before them, sweeping aside the traces of spilled oporto that remained alone to tell of the former officers' interest in the chart.

On the deck of the *Escarabajo de Plata* a lookout called excitedly and pointed into the black sky at an object nearly on line with the deck of the galleon. "Sail ho," he cried, "Sail ho!"

Sailors gathered around to follow his pointing finger and see, moving slowly in the distance, the tiny shape of a craft propelled by spinning paddle wheels, its twin smokestacks giving off little clouds of dense black smoke. Crossing the ether from that distance they could barely hear its steady, cheerful sound: *chuf-chuf-chuf*.

Below decks El Raton and The Skull sat facing each other across a chart table. The words from the lookout smote their ears simultaneously, provoking similar wicked smiles upon the two ill-made countenances.

"A toast, Mister Skull," snarled El Raton Miguelito reaching for the bottle of oporto which stood beside the chart table on a wooden sideboard. The Skull picked up two goblets and held them ready to receive the blood-red liquid.

"To our first foray into piracy," El Raton Miguelito snarled.

CHAPTER 13
A Problem of Largeness

"O Professor," wailed Herkimer, tears streaming down his innocent cheeks in little rivulets that puddled and dripped from his trembling chin onto the rumpled front of his Jeshaw Callister tweed jacket, "now are we truly lost! Not only are we caught in this uncharted region of space, surrounded upon a strange planet by a nation of talking pussycats, but our wonderful etherflyer has been stolen by the rascally Jefferson!

"Never again will I taste the beef pies of my Mother, nor feel the strong if misguided influence of my Dad. Never again shall I pedal my wheel, of which I am so proud, along the sycamore-roofed and gingerbread-lined streets of dear old Buffalo Falls, nor stride the gaslit corridors of the Normal School, joshing and larking it about with my fellows!

"Never again shall I meet with my friends at the Buffalo Falls Young Men's Christian Association to lollygag about on a lazy summer's day, nor escort the estimable Miss Lucille von der Lucans to Revolutionary Park on a Sunday afternoon following services presided over by the Rev. Goodspeed!

"Never again shall we—either of us—set foot upon the sacred soil of our beloved Potawatamy County! O Professor, mentor and friend, why did we ever leave our homes?"

With this piteous oration, delivered in company of facial expressions and manual gesticulations carefully learned in the dramatic declamation syllabus of Professor Thintwhistle, poor Herkimer collapsed into a renewed freshet of tears.

With former king Al looking on in sympathy and the gruff-exteriored Purrfurr sniffing haughtily (but indicating with a softness of eye that his heart was far less rock-like than he would have preferred the generality of catdom to believe) Professor Thintwhistle thought for a moment, the stump of his bitten-off briar clenched tightly in his teeth, then began to address his youthful companion. What thoughts occupied the *savant*'s gray-covered cranium at this moment we know not, although we have in the past detected most puzzlingly unkind notions upon his part as directed toward Herkimer, but at this juncture his words were of the most understanding.

"Dear child," he began, extending his left foot with toe pointed, ankle controlled and knee bent slightly to provide flexibility and freedom of action, "we are, as you would aptly express matters, indeed up against a most difficult situation. But all is not as black as you surmise, nor our situation as hopeless as you have painted it."

Thrusting one hand forward toward the lad, palm up, fingers extended in the position designed to express hopefullness mingled with sympathetic concern, the stump of his ruined briar removed from between his powerful jaws and jammed uncaringly into a pocket, the pedagogue went on, "We find ourselves among an intelligent and seemingly friendly race, whose society appears adequately advanced that they may prove able to assist us in our hour of distress.

"We have further made the acquaintance of Captain

Lupe y Alvarado and obtained from him the promise
of assistance in the event of his finding his own way.
And still further there remains our own servant and
our own ship, for the shiftless darky, upon encounter-
ing the responsibilities of proceeding unguided by superior minds, is likely to return for us, filled with con-
trition at the rashness of his deserter's cowardice. In
which case," said the Professor with a wry expression
and laying a finger archly aside his nose, "we must
pretend to have experienced no inconvenience whatever, but to forgive generously and return the rebel-
lious chap to his own position within the orderly
household of the *Chester Alan Arthur*.

"So buck up, my lad," concluded the Professor, "all
will yet be saved, and not by the mercy of any super-
natural providence, but, as Bishop Brown would put it,
by the diligent application of human intelligence and
hard work!"

So impressed was Herkimer by the eloquence of the
Professor and the message of hope which he expressed, that the lad fell to his knees before the *savant*
and, throwing his arms wide in gesture of acceptance
of the elder person's exhortation, exclaimed, "Fool that
I was to lose faith! But tell me what to do, dear Professor, and it shall be as a thing done!

"Already do I taste my Mother's pumpkin-and-boy-
senberry tarts, already can I hear the fellows exclaiming in wonder and envy as I narrate the tale of our
wondrous adventure, already can I see the pure blue
of Miss von der Lucans' eyes as they gaze admiringly
at us both and at the returned ether-flyer, while Jefferson bustles in his pantry preparing us all a celebratory
feast!"

"Now, now, lad," said the Professor, patting Herkimer kindly upon the top of his head (for the lad had

removed his straw skimmer already in token of respect
for the pedagogue), "a long and winding road winds
ahead ere we see the green hills and bubbling streams
of Potawatamy County again. But see them we shall,
never fear.

"Now, upon your feet, for we must be about the
business of obtaining the cooperation of these cat folk
whose world we visit."

Surveying the region in which they had landed, the
Professor and Herkimer noted that the entire convoy
of felines who had made the airy journey from Felisia
aleph to Felisia beth had landed safely and in comfort.
Purrfurr and former king Al stood by, the cat philosopher pointedly examining the claws of one foot while
the ex-monarch sat gazing at "Old Tut" and "Herk"
with a bland expression on his orange-mottled physiognomy.

"Dear feline friends and fellow travelers from afar,"
the Professor addressed the two cats, pridefully making mental note to remember his clever alliteration
and use it in making his own report of the wondrous
journey to the County Scientific Society, "you are thoroughly familiar with the difficulty in which my young
companion and I find ourselves. Do you not think it
would be apt for us to make our way to the palace of
the local ruler in order that we might deliver our plea
for assistance in finding our way home?"

The two cats acceded to this request, the creamy-
coated Al ambling familiarly beside Professor Thintwhistle, his gaze mildly cast at this object and that,
while the feline *savant* Purrfurr strode ahead, grumbling continuously in a semi-unintelligible manner
such that only an occasional word emerged to the au-
dition of his three companions: "Foolish . . . lost . . . in-
competent . . . only their just desserts . . . huge, clumsy

beasts . . . without grace or good sense," and so on, to
the point that Professor Thintwhistle was forced to
restrain himself from delivering a hearty kick to the
tailless rump of the haughty Manx.

In a while the mixed quartet of humans and cats approached the city limits of Fritzburg, where the unassuming former monarch Al explained mildly to a cere-
monial guardian of the city gates their need to visit
the palace of King Clement. The gatesman, resplen-
dent in the doublet and tights of the colorful past nodded his helmeted head and lowered his pennoned pike-
staff, indicating to the four that they were free to enter
the city.

Both Al and Purrfurr, having previously visited Felisia beth and its royal capital of Fritzburg, took turns
leading the way through the crowded and twisting
streets of the city, explaining to the Professor and Herkimer the many points of local interest which they
passed. Colors ran riot in the architecture of the city
and the fur and garb of the inhabitants who, being
provided by a generous nature with a coating adequate to meet the demands of both warmth and modesty, needs adorn themselves with clothing only as the
decorative urge moved them to do.

Yarn shops were numerous in the streets of
Fritzburg, whose many fine edifices were noted with
admiration by Al, in contrast with the vociferous
sneers of Purrfurr, who drew in all cases unfavorable
contrast with the equivalent features of Catterstall, the
chief city of Felisia beth.

As the quartet passed a catnip shop situated on one
street 'twixt a beauty salon catering to milady's vanity
and a restaurant of slight attractiveness, a gray tabbie
was seen reeling most disgracefully from the establishment wherein was vended the locally favored intoxi-

cant and, as the tabbie staggered into the street and observed the two humans advancing down its center, engaged in obviously sociable converse with the short-hair and the Manx, the poor besotted tabbie turned tail, giving vent to a terrified shriek, which he followed with the words, "Now I'm seein' giants and talkin' monsters right in the streets o' Fritzburg! I musta had one nip too many! Never again! I'm swearin' off! I'm goin' on the wagon! No more catnip for me!"

With a lurch the poor fellow stumbled around a corner and was lost to the sight of the four, although his voice could be heard growing more and more faint with distance. The cats and their human visitors laughed heartily at the plight of the poor catnip-fiend, Purrfurr averring that the tipsy citizen would have a hard time on the following day reconciling his recollections with what he thought to be the limits of reality.

Professor Thintwhistle acquainted his hosts with the facts of the earthly equivalent of catnip, delivering to them a lecture on the virtues of temperance which concluded, "and yet, used in moderation and kept as a friend rather than a master, John Barleycorn can be as pleasant and unassuming a companion as one may wish!"

At this juncture the companions reached the Royal Palace of Fritzburg, where the former king of Felisia aleph was immediately recognized by the chamberlain on duty, and the four were ushered without delay into the audience chamber of King Clement VII of Felisia beth.

The four made themselves comfortable, the Professor resuming his posture of yogic meditation upon a cushion placed on the floor of the chamber, Herkimer clumsily but with good spirit attempting to duplicate the position of his leader, the two cats lapsing into positions of typical feline grace.

Before more than a few minutes had passed the great door of the chamber was opened and a seneschal advanced to stand beside the throne cushion, whence he announced to the four visitors, "His Royal Majesty Clement VII, King of Felisia beth, Ruler of the Planetary Waters, Co-Monarch of the Interplanetary Ether, the Puissant, the Glorious, the Just!"

King Clement strode into the chamber, surveying the four visitors to his domain. The monarch was of black and white configuration, a snow-face with brilliant golden eyes yielding to black ears and a black crest, his body black and glistening save for a white blaze upon the royal chest and graceful markings upon the legs and tail.

As Clement moved to the front of the audience chamber the four visitors made to kneel in deference to his royal prerogatives, but the monarch of Felisia beth waved all to a more comfortable position save the former king of Felisia aleph, whom he embraced heartily, crying out, "Dear cuz, we are overjoyed to see you once again, but how came you to Transfer when you might have remained upon aleph and held onto your crown?"

"The cares of state, my Liege," replied the other, stepping back and admiring the splendid appearance of King Clement, "are such that one is not reluctant to relinquish them when one may do so with honor. What was more, knowing that the great majority of my subjects would be traveling to Felisia beth to become subjects of yours, I could not but accompany them during the Transfer.

"And so I stand before you, plain Mr. Albert Smythe, gentlecat."

The monarch of Felisia beth had by now moved to his throne cushion and seated himself there, his large and furry tail majestically circling his feet. "Dear Cousin," he said formally, "we do hold your person in such affection that you and your party are welcome at our court whatever the time, yet we sense somehow that you have come here with more purpose than the passing of social pleasantries. In view of the severe demands upon our royal time, might we urge that you speak directly to the point of the audience."

Before Al Smythe could speak the advisor Purrfurr spoke up, giving a brief version of Professor Thintwhistle and Herkimer's own tale of travel and of their present problem. "Would Your Majesty be so kind," Sir Purrfurr concluded, "as to provide these travelers with the use of a Felisian coldopter for the purpose of pursuing their errant servant and recovering their own space craft?"

King Clement listened to the story with great concentration, moving his eyes from one to another of his guests during Purrfurr's narration but holding them rivetted for the most part to Professor Thintwhistle or to Herkimer, as if to read their very character written upon their earthly countenances.

At the end of Purrfurr's peroration the cat monarch unfurled his tail, gave a majestic twitch, then resettled it about his royal rump, circling to cover his feet from the direction opposite to that it had previously taken. "We find your tale, Sir Purrfurr, of the greatest interest, and may we say, of so far-fetched a nature that we would be inclined to doubt its veracity but for the presence before our very eyes of the two giants.

"May we ask them to display their remarkable powers of feline-like speech and mentation?" he asked. "The less hirsute one first, if you please."

"Mm, mmum-uhm," stammered Herkimer, "ah, I, ah, em hem-a-hem, ahm, umm." He lapsed into silence blushing furiously.

"Well then," snapped the King, "if this is some sort of elaborate joke, cousin . . ." And with this he glared at the mild-mannered Al, who proceeded to shed white fur in the King's audience chamber.

"I apologize, sir, for my associate's momentary inability to speak," said Professor Thintwhistle, drawing immediately the attention of the monarch and the two other cats in the room.

There was a gasp at the Professor's daring thus to speak, but Clement signalled him to continue.

"In our homeland we have done away with kings, you see, and the people are free to rule themselves, placing such persons in authority as they select, and dispensing with them in favor of others when they see fit to do so. Young Herkimer, here, may have been so awed at the command of a real king that he was momentarily robbed of his powers of speech. Give the lad but a moment's reprieve and I can assure you that he will indeed speak."

At the assenting nod of the king, Professor Thintwhistle turned to young Herkimer and said "Go on, lad, don't be afraid." He bent and whispered something unintelligble in the boy's ear, whereupon Herkimer giggled fetchingly and nodded agreement with the *savant*.

"Greetings, sire," Herkimer said to the king. "I trust that I may now dispel any doubts which Your Highness harbors with regard to my ability of speech. If not, however, I am prepared to continue to speak until such time as Your Majesty is convinced. I may orate upon the virtues of Potawatamy County, Pennsylvania, or upon the workings of the democratic system of government, the laws of natural philosophy as taught to me in the halls of the Buffalo Falls Normal School by none other than the gentleman whom you observe at my side. I may recite the order of finish of teams in the National Baseball League, from its inception by the Cincinnati Red Stockings until the close of the 1883 season, with notations as to batting, running, and pitching performances of outstanding merit. I can recite the names of the Presidents of the United States from Washington through the elegant Arthur, or . . ."

At this point Clement cut him off with a gesture and a distinctly feline hiss. "Enough!" he snapped. "We are convinced." The king rose to his feet, the others in the room following his example as was expected as a matter of etiquette in the presence of royalty.

"Dear Cousin Albert," the cat monarch said, "and you, learned Manxman, will convey our great visitors to the royal aerodrome and permit them to witness an exhibition to be put on this day by the Herriman Escadrille. At the termination of the exhibition, using this token of our royal command—" and he pulled one of his own splendid whiskers with a sudden whisking movement "—you will procure for them a coldopter, to be used as they find needful, and returned to the royal aerodrome at their earliest convenience."

He handed the whisker to the mild-mannered Al, who began quietly to weep in gratitude for his friends. "Now, now," said the monarch, patting Mr. Smythe upon his feline shoulder, "tend to such business as is apropos, and then return, dear cousin, for dinner with Queen Krazy and myself."

The cream sniffled once more, bowed to his reigning cousin, and, with Purrfurr in the lead, the four left the chamber, the audience at its end.

The Fritzburg Royal Aerodrome was a large and impressive structure featuring recreations of great feline aviators of the past in bas relief upon its exterior surfaces. Beside each was a representation of the especial design associated with each pioneer.

Professor Thintwhistle, Herkimer, Al and Purrfurr were seated upon the highest tier of a bleacher facing the aerodrome, surrounded by a large crowd of curious but friendly Felisians. The Professor, whose keen interest in the science of aeronautics should by now be obvious to the reader, found himself fascinated by the analogs apparent betwen Felisian and terrestrial aeronautical history, calling off for the benefit of Herkimer the names of the earthly equivalents of the cat nation's aerial pioneers: Sartey and Cayley's revolving wing experiments, Henson's giant fan-tailed effort, the designs of Siemens, Stringfellow, Jean-Marie La Bris, du Temple, Butler and Edwards, Pomes de la Pauze, Thomas Moy and Tatin.

At length the hangar door was drawn aside and a Royal Felisian coldopter bearing the insignia of the Herriman Escadrille was wheeled onto the flat area before the admiring eyes of an applauding crowd. "You see," explained Purrfurr to the Professor and Herkimer, "that the flying ship is powered entirely by the principle of temperature contrasts.

"Powerful cooling units are placed between its sets of struts, mounted upon rotatable gimbals. The helmsman of the coldopter directs these units in the desired direction of movement—up or down, left or right—whereupon they project a field of intense etheric chill in the direction toward which they were pointed. By the well-known principles of shrinkage or expansion in proportion to the presence of heat energy, the ether is caused to contract in the desired direction, causing the formation of a partial etheric vacuum into which surrounding ether, and the coldopter itself, are drawn.

"By varying the intensity of the cold field projected by the cooling units, the helmsman of the coldopter also controls the speed of movement of the craft. The more intense the cold field, the more powerful the etheric vacuum created and the greater the speed of movement of the coldopter toward the center of the field."

The Herriman Escadrille coldopter had now reached a position on the runway and was preparing to rise into the air. Professor Thintwhistle said, "My dear Purrfurr, your explication of the functional principles of the Felisian colopter is lucid and intriguing, but I wonder as to the source of power of the cold-field generators."

"The generators, my dear colleague," explained Purrfurr, warming to the technical exchange, "are powered by the very fields they create. As you are doubtless aware, heat is energy and the extraction of heat, which is merely another way of saying the generation of cold, involves the removal of energy from the substance being cooled. The heat energy removed from the ether is used to power the cold-field generators, the surplus energy being stored in batteries which are used, when the coldopter returns to its base, for a variety of industrial and personal heating and energy purposes."

"Marvelous!" exclaimed the gray-bearded *savant*, jamming the stub of his shattered briar into his mouth and concentrating his gaze upon the Felisian coldopter, whose name *Frigidia* was blazoned upon her bow. The helmsman revved up his cooling units, a thin powdering of snow began to form as if by a miracle before the power units, and the *Frigidia* began to roll forward.

The occupants of the bleacher huddled together at the sudden wave of chill which passed over them as the *Frigidia* rolled by, but quickly the coldopter became airborne, rising almost vertically overhead. She performed a series of intricate aerial maneuvers, looping, rolling and diving, moving gracefully and at speeds ranging from the barely discernible to the breathtaking, then finally rose straight overhead and disappeared.

"Where has she gone?" Herkimer asked

"She will orbit the three planets of Felisia one time, a matter of assuring that all is well following the late Transfer, then return here and land," replied the mild-mannered Al.

In a short while the coldopter appeared once again overhead, lowered itself gracefully to the landing field, and disgorged her crew who returned to their hangar midst a hearty burst of applause from the bleacher, which thereupon began to empty.

Carefully bearing the whisker of Clement, the party of Al, Purrfurr, Professor Thintwhistle and Herkimer advanced across the field to examine the *Frigidia* at close range.

Kneeling beside the marvelous coldopter, young Herkimer gave vent to a cry of alarm. "She is a beautiful ship," exclaimed the lad, "and performed nobly for her cat crew. But she barely reaches the elastic cuffs of my knicker bottoms. How can she possibly be of use to human occupants?"

CHAPTER 14
Felisian Science's Solution

"My, my," commiserated Al Smythe, his mild blue eyes filled with sympathetic regard for the earthly visitors to Felisia, "the young giant indeed has a point. I fear that you giants could never fit into a Felisian coldopter. Perhaps our manufactures could build a very large coldopter, adapted to the scale of the two of you, so that you could seek out your erring servant."

"Doubtless they could," put in Purrfurr, "but the time required to prepare oversize blueprints, machine tools, and parts, plus the time required to assemble and test such a super-coldopter would be very long. Their ship and servant might be untraceably lost by the time they were prepared to set out on their pursuit.

"But there is another way," the feline philosopher went on, holding one white paw in the air for attention and emphasis in a manner not wholly unlike that used by Professor Thintwhistle himself. "There is another way," he repeated, "if the giants are willing to risk grave injury or death!"

"What is it, Sir?" asked the Professor gravely. "Rather than remain stranded here indefinitely—for all that the Felisian planets are a fascinating and beautiful example of the variety of celestial creation, and the

Felisians lavish and considerate hosts—still, we would accept any risk to bring the rascally Clay to answer for his conduct, following which, it is devoutly to be hoped, we may yet find a way back to the planet of our birth, there to report to our fellows on the wonders we have encountered away from that fertile globe."

"Well, then, if you wish to know all, I shall conceal nothing," stated Purrfurr. "Come with me and I shall explain my plan in some place of privacy."

So saying he led the way to a secluded corner within the Herriman Escadrille hangar, and proceeded to deliver the following oration:

"My friend Mr. Smythe, Professor, young person, as you are no doubt aware modern science has developed a theory of matter which posits the existence of two broad categories of atoms, those of ash and those of phlogiston. Thus we see that when an object is subjected to extreme heat, this loosens the atomic bonds so that the atoms of phlogiston are released, and exit from the area in the form of flame, smoke, or other such effluvia, while the atoms of ash remain behind. Had we the right knowledge of technique, we might recombine the phlogiston, had we captured it in evaporation-tight vessels in the first place. But even so, we know that the weight of the escaping phlogiston, be it positive or negative, can be calculated easily by weighing the whole object prior to combustion and then again weighing its ash. The difference in weight is accounted for by the escaped phlogiston, and in most cases though far from all, the remaining ash is both lighter and more compact than was the original object.

"What I propose to do, Professor and young creature, is subject you both to a process of my own devising and as yet undisclosed to the generality of the Felisian scientific community due to its experimental nature and to my not as yet having obtained a patent upon it, which process will separate your phlogiston from your bodies, leaving intact the atomic relationships of the remainder of your substance.

"I will retain your phlogiston in carefully sealed and labeled containers here in Felisia, while you, having surrendered the phlogiston, will be sufficiently reduced in size and weight as to be able easily to enter and operate the *Frigidia*. Upon the accomplishment of your purpose in regaining possession of your own vehicle, you need but return to Felisia and have restored to you your phlogiston, and, with it, your original dimensions."

Professor Thintwhistle accepted the plan put forth by Purrfurr with the greatest of eagerness, as much so at the exciting scientific prospect of experiencing the experimental removal of his phlogiston as he was at the thought of regaining control of the *Arthur* and bringing Jefferson Jackson Clay to answer for his peculation.

Herkimer, after the briefest of hesitation, followed the lead of his teacher, the pact being sealed with a mutual shaking of the hands of the two humans and the forepaws of Al and Purrfurr. In short order the Felisian philosopher, assisted by his former liege Mr. Smythe, had assembled the materials and equipment needful for the phlogiston experiment and burned a scrap of wood to a fine gray ash as a test.

Satisfied that the apparatus was functioning as had been planned, Purrfurr called upon the two visitors for a volunteer as to who would first undergo the extraction of his phlogiston, which call was immediately responded to by Professor Thintwhistle, who said, "In deference to the youthful impetuosity of my friend and student Herkimer, I shall appoint him to undergo the extraction while I selflessly restrain my own eagerness to experience this new state of being."

"Nay," cried Herkimer, perspiration appearing on his brow and his knees beginning to tremble in a manner more expected of the dusky cabin boy than it was of a star student of the Buffalo Falls Normal School. "I will make that sacrifice, Professor, and permit you to precede me!"

"Do as you are told, Herkimer," exclaimed "Old Tut," giving the youth a smart kick in the seat of his Jeshaw Callister corduroy britches that drove him into the position prepared for the subject of each experiment. Before Herkimer could protest further, Purrfurr and Mr. Smythe were upon him with straps which they affixed while the Professor, a sturdy and well-muscled person despite the graying of his hair and the passage of years, held him unable to move.

At last the three sprang back, Purrfurr threw a switch, and Herkimer, a look of terror in his eyes, began to wither and shrink! Smaller and smaller he grew, his protests growing tinier as did his stature, while an indicator upon a dial set before the Felisian Purrfurr moved upward, indicating the filling of the phlogiston-container, a large globe of transparent construction which, without giving other visible sign of fullness, caused a spring-scale upon which it rested to sink appreciably lower on its base.

By the time the process had ceased Herkimer had shrunk far beneath the size of his bonds, and leaped upon the experimenting table with a cry of gladness at having come through the unprecedented experience in safety.

Professor Thintwhistle permitted himself now to be

led to the table, where he submitted unresistingly to the ministrations of the Felisians, emerging unscathed a few moments later reduced to the size of a common house cat, as had been Herkimer.

The four participants in the bizarre experiment stood for a moment, congratulating one another upon their mutual success and the safety of the two humans, when they were startled to hear, emerging from a voluminous pocket in the Professor's brocaded waistcoat, a small wail of feline distress. It was Cleopatra, who had spent the entire time since their landing upon Felisia beth in the Professor's pocket, and who had now been reduced to the size of a common shrew!

Laughing heartily at the distress of the tiny cat, Mr. Smythe reached into a cupboard nearby and retrieved a small sweet meat which he presented ceremoniously to Cleopatra, the latter accepting the gift and subsiding into a contented purring within the warm shelter of her pocket.

The four experimenters now marched across the field to the still ready *Frigidia*, the Felisians presenting the whisker of Clement VII to the guards as evidence of royal authority. After shaking hands (and paws) all around once again, the two cats bade the humans goodbye and the latter climbed aboard the coldopter.

The interior of the Felisian craft was of course unfamiliar to Professor Thintwhistle and Herkimer, and its appliances designed and built for the use of Felisian rather than human occupants, so that although the Professor and his acolyte were now of the proper size to operate the coldopter, they found its furnishings and controls most strange. Many minutes were required for the Professor fully to familiarize himself with the *Frigidia*'s operating instruments, but after a time he felt himself adequately qualified and, setting the

directional control of the cooling units, or cold generators, to accomplish a smooth and gradual rise from the
ground, he waved through one window to the still
watching Purrfurr and Al, slid the intensity lever forward one third of the way to its fullest setting, and exhaled with satisfaction as the coldopter rose from the
Felisian surface, nosing through a miniature blizzard
of its own making.

With Herkimer hovering anxiously at his elbow, and
with the stump of his brittle briar clenched between
his teeth, the Professor circled first the Herriman
Escadrille aerodrome, then the city of Fritzburg,
buzzing the royal palace to leave a trail of snow across
its grounds and roof, then rose high above the atmosphere of Felisia beth and set the coldopter into a
course that drove her looping among the three planets
of the Felisian group.

As the *Frigidia* circled above the half-deserted
globe of Felisia aleph Herkimer cried out "Look, mentor, through the window! Tis a trail of slowly dissipat-
ing cloudlets of smoke from the *Arthur*'s stacks! We
have found the trail of the errant Jefferson and our
purloined ether-flyer!"

"Indeed we have," confirmed the *savant*, casting a
gimletlike glance through the window indicated by
his follower, upon which statement the simple Herkimer burst into a jolly celebratory jig and cries of
"Huzzah! Huzzah! We shall yet be saved!"

The Professor tolerated this conduct for a reason-
able period of time, then assigned Herkimer to a routine task in the interior of the *Frigidia*, thereby removing him from the immediate area of the helmsman's
post and keeping him from his usual custom of annoy-
ing the pedagogue.

Professor Thintwhistle swung the helm of the *Fri-*

gidia now this way and now that, turning the cold-field projectors attached to the exterior of the craft in various directions, at length homing in upon the trail of the *Arthur's* exhaust and sliding the intensity level slowly forward until it was at the fullest extent of his track.

The *Frigidia* moved forward now at increasing acceleration, the reduced-energy pockets ahead of its projectors growing colder and colder, more and more vacuum-like, thereby causing the coldopter to race ever more rapidly into them. Here in the transplanetary void there was of course only ether to be encountered, rather than moisture-bearing air, so that the snow of the atmospheric flight was absent, although as each puff of the *Arthur's* anthracitic exhaust was subjected to the coldopter's cooling units it precipitated into a Stygian sort of dust.

As the *Frigidia* increased her pace from the sedate speed at which she had swooped gracefully through the atmosphere of Felisia beth to greater and greater levels, her two-man crew of captain and helper were impressed by the many interesting sights to which they were witness through the windows of the coldopter, sights which Herkimer, finding the Felisian equivalent of foolscap and stylus among the supplies of the ship, proceeded to record in the manner of which he was best capable.

The multitude of stars and lesser celestial objects visible about the swiftly proceeding coldopter seemed to shift in position and tone, those ahead of the swift-moving craft appeared to draw more and more closely packed, their tints altering subtly into a rosy magenta hue while those behind the speeding ship seemed to draw apart and away, even the brilliant disk of Taphammer receding to a single dazzling point in the firmament, while their tones drew farther and farther toward a pale mauve.

Onward drove the sleek *Frigidia,* her cold-field generators drawing ever more energy from the ether in which she had her being, the partial ether-vacuums ahead of the generators becoming increasingly devoid of the universal fluid, the nacelles of the generators themselves becoming encrusted with superfrigidified particiles of carbon-anthricite exhaust from the fleeing *Arthur,* the whole intermixed with such fragments of interstellar flotsam as chanced to be caught in the cooling sweep of the Frigidia's generators.

This was the first time that the *Frigidia* or, for that matter, any Felisian coldopter had penetrated the cosmic void beyond the planetary family for the friendly star Taphammer, but the fineness of Felisian technology and the extreme care of the mechanicians associated with the Herriman Escadrille and the entire establishment of the court of King Clement VII of Felisia beth had assured that the ship would perform to perfection in even the most trying of circumstances.

As for Professor Theobald Uriah Thintwhistle and his assistant and fellow traveler Herkimer, there was little lacking in the provision of necessities for the comfortable journey of either. Even the radical reduction in their bodily dimensions through the removal of their phlogiston at the hands of the Felisian Purrfurr was of little momentary concern, for each had been reduced in perfect proportion to his former size, and each, further, had maintained his appropriate relationship to the other, the grizzled Professor being as wide and brawny a figure as ever he had been, proportionately speaking, and the lad Herkimer being still as gawky and gangling a figure as he had hitherto presented on the streets and byways of Buffalo Falls.

Even little Cleopatra had recovered from her experience in the phlogiston-removal device, and had commenced to scamper about the interior of the *Frigidia* as gaily and with as much playfulness as she had customarily manifested in the *Arthur*. Her kittens, she knew, were by now well adapted to food which Jefferson might provide from the *Arthur*'s ships stores, and though Cleo might well yearn with the warmth of the universal instinct of maternity for contact with her furry offspring, still she was well content in her instinctive understanding of their safety.

The relative tranquility of the cabin of the *Frigidia* was broken in time by the appearance of more remarkable visual effects than those seen at any previous time. The heavenly illumination in which the tiny ship had basked since leaving the immediate locale of shining Taphammer had convinced Professor Thintwhistle of the temporary superfluity of using the ship's own lighting, which he had doused, permitting the interior of the craft to be bathed in a variety of tints of starry illumination which, upon arriving from its many and far distant sources, was permitted freely to pass through the sealed windows of the coldopter and to bathe its interior in its greatly varied tones.

Now the sources of illumination commenced to dance and wink, the whole thus presented offering to the wondering eyes of "Old Tut" and "Herk" a sight of such unprecedented splendor that no effort was made to switch on the interior illumination of the ship; rather, the controls were so set that the cold-field generators would continue to draw the ship along the trail left by the fleeing *Arthur*, while the *Frigidia*'s tiny crew sat upon comfortable cushions, gazing raptly at the show being provided by Mother Nature in the universe beyond their cabin.

Now shafts and spirals of color, suggestive of *aurora borealis* but far surpassing that nocturnal phenomenon, appeared to the eyes of the thrilled travelers. The Professor and his student sat with legs crossed, eyes glued to the windows, watching the play of greens and golds, blue, purple, red and pink, yellows and ultramarines, across the face of the cosmic presence.

At length, fearing that the monstrous speed built up by the accelerating coldopter would cause it to overtake and either bypass or crash through the more slowly moving *Chester A. Arthur,* the Professor rose from his cushion and resumed his position at the controls of the *Frigidia,* sliding back the lever which controlled the intensity of the cold fields projected by her cooling units, so that the ship was slowed gently by her uncounted tiny collisions with spatial particles of the *Arthur's* exhaust and other miniature bits of leftover (or incipient) creation as might cross her still rapidly pursued progress.

At this very moment, while the *Frigidia* pursued the newly rechristened ether-flyer *Crispus Attucks* through the stretches of the interstellar void beyond the star Taphammer, and while the newly reorganized pirate crew of the Tsarist Iberian galleon *Escarabajo de Plata* witnessed the approach of the same *Crispus Attucks,* the former *Chester Alan Arthur,* with greedy anticipation of their first filibustering foray, vitally related activities were under way in the normally sleepy and untroubled town of Buffalo Falls, ofttimes known to her admirers as the Pearl of Potawatamy County.

Night had fallen in that bucolic community, and in a certain tranquil residential neighborhood where the well-regulated lives of the local inhabitants had long since seen them safely behind their own doors and into fleece-quilted beds of mahogany or brass, there flared in one cellar a flickering illumination cast by carefully trimmed gaslights. The room was located beneath ground level, with only a narrow row of earth-level windows threatening to betray the presence therein of any persons, and even these windows were carefully shrouded in darkly opaque cloths, so that any stray constable, or even Sheriff Jeshaw Callister making an evening patrol following the locking and barring of his nonpareil dry goods emporium, would detect no activity from within the Thintwhistle domicile.

For the house of which we speak was indeed the white-coated, gingerbread-trimmed home of the beloved professor of natural philosophy and dramatic declamation, himself far away at the moment of which we speak.

Within the cellar workroom of the Professor, her thin and bony back bent over a battered and ancient desk formerly used by the owner of the house for the placement of his blueprints and notebooks, the indefatigable Miss Olivia Taphammer, embattled music mistress of the Buffalo Falls Normal School, studied the papers deserted by the Professor at the time of his departure with Jefferson and Herkimer in the *Chester A. Arthur.*

Behind the music mistress Mr. Winchester Blount, instructor in geography, paced fretfully back and forth, his pink and neatly manicured hands fluttering in agitation as he pleaded with his companion to quit the premises before they should be discovered by the minions of the town powers.

"It is not merely that we may be accused of breaking and entering, Miss Taphammer," he quavered, "it is far more than the possibility of facing that criminal charge, of which I am sure we would be cleared in the light of our attempts to locate the missing trio. It is the indelible taint of scandal which would inevitably accrue to us both were we found unchaperoned in a locked and deserted house and at night!"

A shudder of apprehension shook the fleshy frame of the geographer.

"Oh, flute valves and fiddlesticks, Mr. Blount," Miss Taphammer exclaimed, "let the old busybodies and their biddy wives gossip all they please. We know we are doing nothing improper here, and even if we were, of whose concern is it other than our own?"

"But the school board, Miss Taphammer. And the ministerial alliance. The Rev. Goodspeed is a powerful member of both, and you know how unsympathetic he is to the idea of your presence on the Normal School faculty to begin with."

"Dear Winchester," Miss Taphammer said, turning from the work before her and facing her colleague with her hands on her hips, "I do not know very much about Pastor Goodspeed's alleged mind, nor do I care very much. What I am interested in is the whereabouts of Professor Thintwhistle and the two young men who disappeared with him, and if you will only be so good as to attend to the task at hand, I believe that we shall be able to find those three individuals when no one else in this town apparently cares enough even to look for them!

"Now listen carefully, for to the crime of breaking and entering Professor Thintwhistle's house this night, we are going to add the crimes of breaking, entering, and theft at the establishments of no lesser lights than the mayor and the sheriff."

"Oh dear, oh dear, oh oh dear dear me!" wailed Mr. Blount "into what have I gotten myself!"

"Do you wish to withdraw from our joint endeavor, Mr. Blount?"

"No, Miss Taphammer, I suppose I had as well be hanged for a sheep as for a lamb. What is your plan?"

CHAPTER 15
Toward Reunions

In the Palace of Peace and Joy, headquarters and royal seat of the Lunite Commonwealth, all was not well. The exterior aspect of the palace and its surrounding grounds was as ever. Rose marble and green jade rose shimmering in the bright rays of old Sol while gold-trimmed spires reflected dazzlingly to the far horizon; dense and exotic shrubbery imported generations earlier from all quarters of the moon by King Lunus himself, after whom the great empire had been named, was kept in perfect trim and gorgeous flower by hereditary gardeners who took great pride in their position.

The Royal Ice Cream Brigade paraded up and down in the courtyard before the main gate of the Palace, while nearby the reflecting pond gave back mirror-perfect images of sky, shrub, and building. Sounds of rippling waters and tinkling chimes filled the faintly perfumed air that surrounded the Palace of Peace and Joy, and in the great Hall of the Arts magnificent paintings shared luxurious galleries with the greatest sculpture in the history of the Lunites.

But still all was not well.

Even the lowliest members of the royal retinue had heard reports and would obligingly add speculation to rumor given half the chance. On the very steps of the

Palace, usually taciturn guardsmen gossiped like women: "I am worried about Her Majesty," the moustachioed Touggourt whispers to his fellows, hoping not to be overheard by his commander. "She has been feverishly flushed today, and places her hand to her brow as if pained."

"She paces as if impatient to be about something, but knows not what she wishes to be about," adds Sulawesi of the jeweled turban. He shakes his own head in puzzlement and concern, dropping a clatter of aquamarines and diamonds upon the marbled floor, where they lie unnoticed until a barefooted ambassador curses the guards; they pick up the offending jewels and stow them more carefully in Sulawesi's turban.

Aguascalientes, a man of normally taciturn bent, chatters nervously. "She snaps at everyone, sending handmaidens in tears and chamberlains in anger from her apartment, then relents and apologizes for her unfair conduct. She orders great meals and sends them away untouched."

The tall and bony Zartaclave rubs his pointed chin meditatively, then speaks. "Ever since she received the wound upon her breast she has been in troubled and unpredictable form. The wound itself seemed to heal rapidly enough, but Selena never recovered her equilibrium."

The guards continue to speculate upon the condition of their monarch, the gravity of their concern reflected in the low tones and sidelong glances that emerge from their conclave.

Within the royal apartment of the Palace of Peace and Joy the object of this concern paced up and down, forehead furrowed, hands clasped behind her naked back. Selena the Queen of the Moon whirled to her chief lady in waiting and snapped, "We are really puzzled over our own mood of late. Something is the matter with us. We feel strange inside, as though the interior architecture of our royal body were unbalanced."

Lady Culicida hid a grin and replied, "Perhaps your majesty is lonely."

"Lonely?" snapped the Queen. "Why do you say that, Culicida? We are surrounded by the usual Palace staff. Why should we suddenly become lonely?"

"I had in mind a special sort of loneliness," the lady in waiting answered, lowering her eyes to a hoop of petit point embroidery upon which she was working.

For a moment the Queen stood as if stunned, then said, "Romantic nonsense, my lady. I am surprised at you for even suggesting it!"

"Perhaps a mere touch of the *malaise,* Your Majesty," suggested a second lady in waiting.

"Thank you, Lady Threnida, but so vague a diagnosis will, we fear, be of little assistance in recovering our usual spirits."

A third lady spoke. "Perhaps a change of scene, or an evening of entertainment to break Your Majesty's mood."

"Ah, Lady Melanopla," said the Queen, visibly brightening, "an evening of entertainment may do well. Our royal thanks for the suggestion!" With one snake-bangled arm Selena reached for a pull-cord of gold-woven rope and tugged at it heavily.

Within moments a chamberlain entered the royal apartment, bowing low to Selena so that the plumes rising from his lavendar turban brushed her royal knees. "Your bidding, Majesty," he said.

"We would be entertained, Nagyszeben. Musicians, flowing wines, dancing boys of the prettiest types, jugglers, fire eaters, whatever you can conjure. We have been off our royal feed lately, and the Lady Me-

lanopla has wisely suggested such a beguilement to restore our royal good cheer and stable disposition."

The chamberlain bowed and backed from the royal
apartment.

As he did so, there in the Palace of Peace and Joy,
royal seat of the Lunite Commonwealth, other events
were moving forward in other places, places which
may have been far away—or close at hand. For the
distance of a trillion miles may be but the difference
between a point in the space with which we are familiar and one adjacent but located in a space with which
we are unfamiliar.

(Author's note: if this puzzles you, just pass over it
and keep the action going. You may understand better
in years to come. Or perhaps you will not.)

In the crow's nest of the *Escarabajo de Plata* the
sailor on duty, a swarthy and ill-kempt fellow known
exclusively and for reasons readily apparent to all acquainted with him as Scar, called a third time to those
on the deck below him, "Sail ho!" The cry was not
strictly an accurate one, to be sure, for the object of
his sight was none other than the *Chester Alan Arthur*,
or, more properly, the *Crispus Attucks*, redubbed such
by her newly self-appointed commanding officer, the
equally renamed Menelik XX Chaka.

The *Attucks* was moving rapidly through the etheric
sea on a course which would bring her near enough to
the *Escarabajo* for the galleon's cannons to terrify her
into submission, or if need be so to batter her that
boarding parties could land with little or no opposi-
tion. For the *Attucks*, although renamed, was still phy-
sically the *Arthur*, a craft built and equipped for the
noble task of peaceful exploration of the space surrounding the earth and her heavenly neighbors, and as
such bore neither armament nor armor save for those

specialized devices smuggled on board by Captain Chaka in his former identity as Jefferson Jackson Clay, houseman, cabin boy, major domo and general facto- tum to the elderly Professor T. U. Thintwhistle.

Even now, within the saloon of the *Attucks*, the *Ar- thur*'s old decor remained with hardly an alteration: the Kermanshahan carpeting, the mahogany wall pan- els, the horsehair-stuffed easy chairs, the smoking stands and antimacassared deal-top tables. Only the portraits of Zaghlul Pasha and the Professor's own Old Dad, Thaddeus Unganno Thintwhistle, while retaining their positions beside the isinglass covered portholes, had been covered over by sheets of foolscap bearing revolutionary slogans considered more appropriate by the new proprietor *de facto* of the ship.

Still, of sails, she bore none.

Upon the Captain's Veranda, Menelik XX Chaka had set his controls to carry the *Crispus Attucks* in a slowly expanding spiral course of exploration, while the Captain himself remained at the main window, folding spyglass in hand, training the instrument now upon this celestial object, now upon that, hoping to make such contact with revolutionary movements or leaders in this new space as would lead to the quick improvement of the oppressed peoples of the local planets as could be achieved, and at the same time as- sist himself in the eventual return to the world of his origin.

The kittens had been fed with good proletarian left- over scraps, the boiler and furnace had been stoked and watered, the Captain had liberated a generous portion of the sherry hoarded by the previous deca- dent administration, and he stood now at his ease gaz- ing through the spyglass, which in turn was leisurely scanning that portion of the heavens ahead of the ship.

Slowly a grin spread across the dusky face of Captain Menelik XX Chaka at the sight of an object that hove into his view, far distant from the *Crispus Attucks* and moving slowly, but nonetheless sailing on an intersecting course. It was none other than the Iberian galleon *Escarabajo de Plata,* captained, Chaka knew, by a man he believed to be sympathetic to his own proletarian sufferings, one whom he believed he could convince of the need to overthrow decadent institutions and substitute for them a revolutionary state of affairs.

Chaka sipped greedily at the bottle of sherry standing at his elbow, returned it to its place, then undogged the controls of the ether-flyer and reset them so that the little craft would be propelled by its great paddle wheels toward the oncoming *Escarabajo* and his own first meeting—as an equal—with Captain Lupe y Alvarado.

The plucky little flyer responded easily to Chaka's skilled hand, a skill gained through many a clandestine hour of study and application in the cellar workroom in Buffalo Falls while Professor Thintwhistle was absent teaching his assemblages at the Normal School or otherwise away from his home.

Now, in the depths of this strange intra-Selenate void, those hours of hard labor were paying generous dividends as Chaka flicked a toggle switch, spun a dial, set a lever, and the *Crispus Attucks'* paddle wheels whirred her on a smooth and steady course, the *chuf-chuf-chuf* of her powerful boilers setting a steady rhythm for the uncontrollable tapping of Captain Chaka's African toes.

In the *Attucks'* spyglass the *Escarabajo* began to grow large, her bellying sails filled with the invisible etheric wind, her pennons streaming from the tops of

her masts, the hydra-headed standard of Tsarist Iberia
fluttering proudly in its brilliant hues. For a while
Chaka watched contentedly, moving only to raise the
bottle of sherry to his broad lips, then to return it to its
position at the edge of the control panel after he had
quaffed a sufficiency of its contents.

But the approach of the two craft was a slow and
barely perceptible matter, and in time the woolly-
pated Chaka grew tired of the sport of watching the
Escarabajo grow. Leaving his controls locked on a
course leading to intersection with the galleon, the
self-appointed Captain strode down the stairway into
the ether-flyer's saloon, carrying with him the folding
spyglass he had removed from the Captain's Veranda.
This, in one hand; in the other, the bottle of sherry.

Upon reaching the Kermanshahan carpeted luxury of
the saloon, Chaka flung himself sprawling into a comfortable armchair, placed his bottle on the nearest
table, and applied his eye once again to the spyglass,
through which, taking his sighting via a saloon window, he was astonished to witness the approach, as
from a great distance behind, of yet a third ship that
plied the etheric seas, a ship as different in appearance
from his own as was that latter, the *Attucks,* from the
slowly approaching galleon *Escarabajo de Plata.*

The new craft was shaped not unlike an elongated
barrel, heavily ribbed along its sides, the protruding
ridges extending from the blunt nose of the strange
machine to its similarly flattened tail. Between the
ridges, mounted so that they appeared to swivel from
time to time while Chaka watched, were a number of
compact devices, presumably propulsion units of a
type, for upon their swivelling the entire odd craft
seemed to proceed in the direction in which the power
units were pointed.

Only the distance between his own ether-flyer and the newcomer puzzled Menelik XX Chaka, for as he focused his spyglass, assuming the ribbed ship to approximate the *Attucks* in size, its outlines grew fuzzy, and as he refocused his spyglass to bring the new ship into sharper view, the indicated range must needs be so small as to make the new craft hardly larger than a good-sized biscuit tin!

Chaka swallowed a goodly mouthful of sherry, wiped his streaming jaws upon an ill-fitting commodore's jacket which he had liberated from the ship's wardrobe for his own use, and rose unsteadily from his chair. He made his way somewhat unsteadily to the Captain's Veranda, checked on the distance yet separating himself from the *Escarabajo*, then stood transfixed as he saw, through the powerful magnifying lenses of the spyglass, the deck hands of the galleon heaving overboard the clearly recognizable bodies of two men!

For several minutes Chaka stood transfixed, watching the drama taking place upon the galleon. For a time men milled about in confusion upon her decks, then there was a rush to a companionway door, a surge back onto the deck, and two more bodies were dumped overboard. In the void of etheric space, the four figures formed a figure of orbiting shapes, slowly revolving around the hull of the *Escarabajo*.

Turning and training his spyglass through the saloon window of the *Attucks*, Chaka could see that the smaller barrel-shaped craft was moving speedily toward him. He pressed the glass close against his eye, and for a moment, through some trickery of the laws of optics, was able to peer through the window of the tiny following craft, and see at her pilot's station none other than his former employer and *bête noire*, Theobald Uriah Thintwhistle! At the Professor's elbow stood the simpleminded ofay boy Herkimer.

Chaka spun to study the galleon *Escarabajo* once more and saw that its crew had hauled down the Tsarist banner and was at this very moment in the act of hoisting in its place the Jolly Roger, dreaded symbol of the deadly buccaneers of ages past!

This was a situation fraught with peril in all quarters. Never before in the course of his brief captaincy had Menelik XX Chaka had to face so difficult a conundrum with regard to his conduct of the affairs of the ship. Ahead of him was a craft but newly taken over by pirates, her captain and his officers, if Chaka guessed a-right, murdered and thrown overboard to orbit their own ship in the depths of the ethereal sea.

Behind him the deposed captain of his own etherflyer, somehow miraculously equipped with a new craft, one seemingly faster and more powerful than the one he had lost, vengeance in his eye and determination in the set of his jaw, fast catching up to the vagrant ship. What should Chaka do? He was a revolutionary commander. He had to act in such a manner as to further the interests of the sacred Movement.

What *could* he do?

Chaka pulled again at the bottle of sherry and, finding that it was now empty, threw it angrily into the earth surrounding the base of a small potted palm that stood to one side of the Captain's Veranda.

"Oobah, joobah, ugga, hogga, bugga, wogga," chanted Chaka, reverting in this moment of stress (and with the assistance of the sherry he had liberated from the ether-flyer's stores) to the ancestral chants with which his forebears had entreated the benevolent intercession of their grotesque and superstition-haunted deities.

Falling into the spirit of his new effort, the former Jefferson Jackson Clay, clad in splendid if ill-fitting braid and trim, trotted up and down on the Captain's Veranda, stood tottering on the edge of the deck, then with a savage whoop leaped to the Kermanshahan carpet that covered the floor of the ship's saloon and burst into a savage dance, hooting and bellowing, stamping and capering about. The kittens scampered for cover behind a chair. The saloon resounded to the African chants and songs of the atavistic Chaka. The very framework of the *Crispus Attucks* seemed to vibrate in time with the leaps and outcries of the hysterical Menelik XX Chaka.

At length Chaka collapsed, panting, onto the Kermanshahan rug, gathered his strength with a mighty effort, and rose to his feet. What dark gods of his ancient people had heard his prayer, what strange Valhalla had answered the pleas of the modern supplicant, we can only guess. No voices were heard in the saloon of the *Crispus Attucks*, no fiery writing illuminated the starry ether, but somehow Chaka knew what he must do.

Striding erratically back to the Captain's Veranda he reset the ether-flyer's controls yet again, so that she would match course with the *Escarabajo*, maintaining such a speed that she should neither lose the galleon nor be overtaken by it, but hold the sailing ship at a constant distance, to be attended to at a later time when the problem of the ribbed space-flyer had been disposed of.

The effort exhausted Menelik XX Chaka momentarily, but after he had sat on the Veranda steps a few seconds he regained his strength and wove dizzily to the rear of the saloon, struggling through the doorway that separated it from his own domain in the rear of the ship. He checked the boilers and furnace to see that all was in good order, then unlocked his battered rolltop desk once again and proceeded to expose a variety of bewildering electronic gear.

As he had once before to the terminal inconvenience of Second Leftenant Blithering-Snipe and his polyglot crew of asteroidal soldiers, the erstwhile Jefferson Jackson Clay set controls and flicked switches that would activate the fatal magnetic trail that would lead the little barrel-ship that pursued the *Attucks* so relentlessly into the ether-flyer's smokestack, down its shaft and into the hungry maw of the fiery furnace, where the troublesome Professor Thintwhistle and his obnoxious acolyte Herkimer would be reduced to crisp bits of blackened ash in a matter of minutes.

For whether it was in that moment of peculiar optical clarity or in the strange period when dark gods of old Africa had somehow seemed to communicate to their latter-day adherent, Chaka was convinced that the barrel ship was hardly larger than an ordinary basketball such as those used at the Normal School where the Professor taught the privileged youth of the decadent town! How he knew this, or how it could be so, Chaka did not know. But somehow, deep in the murky recesses of his primitive but cunning brain, there lurked a perception that had given Chaka access to this terrible and perilous truth.

The black commodore assured himself that the magnetic mechanism was properly adjusted and fully activated, then turned to the nearest porthole and scanned the sky to the rear of the *Crispus Attucks* with his spyglass. There, surely enough, the little ship with the form of a ridged barrel swam into his view, sliding through the etheric void as if on invisible rails, its circle of propulsive units swiveling now this way, now that, as the little craft closed in upon the trail of the *Crispus Attucks*.

And on the coldopter *Frigidia* Professor Thintwhistle stood, bitten-off stump of a briar clenched in his teeth, eyes fixed grimly upon the larger ship which he had himself built with his own hands. Between unmoving jaws he said to his sole crewman Herkimer, "Now comes the time of greatest peril, boy.

"I am painfully aware, and have been since first I faced you as master to pupil in the halls of Buffalo Falls Normal School, that your intellect is of less than outstanding quality. Yet, Herkimer, in the time yet to come I shall have to rely upon your assistance, for we face the prospect of confronting a full-sized Jefferson Jackson Clay in a full-sized *Chester Alan Arthur*, while we are ourselves no larger than ordinary house cats.

"We must somehow regain the obedience of that pesky servant, and cause him to return with us to Felisia beth at the star Taphammer, there to return our borrowed coldopter, regain our temporarily lost phlogiston, and ultimately to resume our search for a way home. It will not be an easy task, nor will—by Jove!" the Professor interrupted himself. "The scoundrel! How dare he! This is too much, far too much!"

"What is it, Professor?" asked Herkimer, a look of dumbfounded puzzlement replacing upon his "phiz" the expression of incomprehending contentment which normally occupied his features. "What has happened?"

"Look, Herkimer," ordered the Professor, pointing through a near-by window (for the two craft had been drawn now into close priximity), "that miscreant has covered over the name of ether-flyer, that of the illustrious Chester Alan Arthur, and painted in its place the words *Crispus Attucks*."

"Sounds like a breakfast cereal to me, Sir," said Her-kimer.

"No, laddy-buck," the Professor responded angrily, "I believe it is the name of some character in the dar-kies' own pantheon. Oh, foul, foul conduct!"

At this point, the plans of the Professor and Her-kimer as yet incomplete, the coldopter *Frigidia* was seized, engines straining futilely to pull her away from the awful magnetism of the *Attucks'* death-trap, and plunged over the crennelated crown that sur-mounted the ether-flyer's main smokestack!

Herkimer screamed in helpless horror.

Professor Thintwhistle silently struggled with the controls of the Felisian ship, spinning the power units about on their gimbals, sliding the intensity control to its highest level, but all to no avail.

The *Frigidia* tumbled over the edge of the smoke-stack, down its black and sooty neck, to strike squarely in the center of the searing flames of finest western Pennsylvania anthracite!

shearing. If they do, perhaps we will permit them to escape with their lives. Ahahahahah!"

The first officer hastened to do his commander's bidding, while Scar, in the crow's nest, watched alternately the strange ship sailing her matched course and the activities taking place on the deck of the *Escarabajo* many feet below his own position.

Watching the preparations of the starboard cannoneers with satisfaction, Scar waited until the cannon were all set up and the fuse of the first alight, then raised his eyes to the proposed target of the shot. At the sight of the foreign ship, Scar began to shout new information to the deck below him, but too late, for 'ere more words than "Ahoy, deck—" had escaped his lips, the *Escarabajo*'s number one starboard cannon had roared smoke and flame and belched her iron shot toward the alien craft.

"Que pasa?" shouted Diaz and Ordaz simultaneously at each the other, "What happened?" For as the galleon's cannon fired her shot, the first such firing since the fateful morning, upon which Captain Lupe y Alvarado, who was still visible in his orbit about the hull of the ship, had failed in his efforts to prevent the *Escarabajo* from sailing over the edge of the earth and into this strange etheric limbo, the ship began to whirl about the long axis of her hull, her masts tipping, her cannons beginning to roll about her deck, her hull rising slowly above her sails.

In the crow's nest, Scar found himself holding to the hemp railing for dear life, lest he be pitched from his post and either tumble to the deck of the ship or fly into space along with the bodies of Captain Lupe y Alvarado, Mister Limon, El Raton Miguelito and The Skull. As Scar clung to the ropes he saw the gunners on deck frantically attempting to get off new shots, ob-

viously thinking that the strange foreign ship had attacked them with a new and terrible weapon causing
them to capsize, but as another shot was got off the
gyration of the *Escarabajo* merely increased, becoming more complex and difficult to deal with as a diag-
onal whirling was added to that already existing.

Gun after gun was gotten off by the galleon's plucky
crewmen, but rather than striking the enemy ship or
serving in any way to offset the *Escarabajo's* own er-
ratic movement, each round served only to accelerate
and render more complex the spinning motion of the
ship. Faster and faster the *Escarabajo* whirled, and
more and more wildly.

Scar collapsed to the floor of the crow's nest, peering out between the hemp railings, looking down to a
scene of madness on the deck as sailors were flung
about, staggering into one another, now lifted off their
feet by the force of the galleon's whirling, now crushed
back onto the deck, now clinging to the rails, the cannon, the lines and masts or simply one another, now
being thrown clear of the *Escarabajo* to swoop madly
through space all around the ship.

At last, unable longer to bear the terrible visions
vouchsafed to his dark Iberian eyes, Scar shuddered
into the lowest possible position within the crow's
nest, clamped straining eyelids shut upon his orbs,
clung with all his strength to the rigging, and began
loudly to recite prayers which had not passed his
swarthy lips since the days long ago in Barcelona
when his sainted mother had taken him regularly to
visit the cathedral.

Even so, it seemed to Scar that the flashing stars and
whirling bodies burned their horrid visions through
his eyelids, the very images searing into his poor, terrified brain. Shrieks of fear tore from his throat, his

every muscle clenched spasmodically, and still, without let or relief, he felt a sudden terrible coldness sweep through him, turning his whole body into a single huge lump of ice. Then, as he lay clenched in frigid and rigid agony a new terror overcame him.

His entire body seemed to be wrenched, twisted, translated through some unknowable dimensional gateway. Gradually the coldness passed, the mad whirling of the *Escarabajo* ceased, and Scar felt a warmly benevolent sun caressing his body with its rays.

He opened his eyes hesitantly and found himself gazing up into a lemon-yellow sky in which a brilliantly blue sun blazed. Turning his eyes downward in puzzlement, Scar saw the decks of the *Escarabajo* totally devoid of human occupants, while a series of distinct splashes drew his attention to the forms of all the *Escarabajo*'s crewmen, even those of Lupe, Limon, El Raton Miguelito and The Skull, tumbling from their positions of flight into the waters upon which the galleon rested quietly. And, to Scar's astonishment, those waters were of a brilliant magenta hue.

As the sailors in the water rose and walked easily across its face, back toward the lines hanging from the rail of the galleon, and began busily to climb back toward her deck, Scar in his crow's nest began quietly to sob into his trembling hands.

At this very moment, far, far away in Buffalo Falls, Pennsylvania, atop the geographical feature known as Revolutionary Hill, a strange and hitherto only once precedented event was being re-enacted.

Inside the cabin of the *Susan B. Anthony,* while Miss Olivia Taphammer carefully guided the near-replica of the original ether-flyer along pathways so that her powered ground-treads did not furrow the neatly tended grass placed by the Potawatamy County Public Works Commission, Mr. Winchester Blount puttered about, marveling at the vehicle which he had helped to construct.

"It was a brilliant stroke on your part to add ground treads to the Professor's blueprints," Mr. Blount said, addressing himself to the taffeta-clad music mistress.

"Merely obvious, Winchester," replied Miss Taphammer, spinning the ether-flyer's helm so that its tracks swung it around the gentle curve at the approach to the hill and began to carry it upward.

"Obvious?" repeated Mr. Blount. "Obvious? How, Miss Taphammer, can you consider this improvement—and, I suppose, the others which you have added to the original plans—to be obvious, when so brilliant and original a mind as that of Professor Thintwhistle failed to take it into consideration in the planning and construction of the *Chester Alan Arthur?*"

"Why, my dear friend, it is clear that you have never worked in a field of invention, such as music or natural philosophy. Perhaps in an area of observation and discovery such as your own, the obvious is the first seen. But in matters of mechanical invention such as the Professor's, it is often the fresh eye of the outside observer that sees the obvious, while that of the inventor himself, so caught up is it in the complex details of his work, very often fails to notice the obvious means for improvement.

"Further," Miss Taphammer continued, "there can be no denying the greatness of Professor Thintwhistle's invention. The improvements which we have installed upon the *Susan B. Anthony* are in fact refinements of relatively trivial significance as compared with the original conception and construction of the ether-flyer."

"I am sure you are right, Miss Taphammer," said Mr. Blount, waving his pink hands in the air as if to mold an atmospheric replica of the thought he was expressing. "But we are now at the crest of the hill," he concluded.

"Very well. Will you join me upon the Veranda to observe our departure from the earth?" Miss Taphammer stood slightly to one side as Mr. Blount climbed the stairway from the saloon to the Captain's Veranda.

As soon as both had stationed themselves before the obvservation windows above the main control panel of the flyer, Miss Taphammer pressed down upon a large switch, slid the newly improved clutchless gear lever into a more forward position, and grasped the helm firmly in her thin but graceful hands.

The *Susan B. Anthony* rolled forward upon her treads, gathering speed steadily as she advanced down Revolutionary Hill. As she moved more and more quickly toward the bottom of the decline in the rich Potawatamy County soil Miss Taphammer drew back upon a vertical control bar and the ether-flyer gracefully rose from the greensward, swooped low over the purling river beyond, then curved about to pass over the town of Buffalo Falls itself.

Then, setting her controls for a gentle but unstinting increase in attitude, Miss Taphammer turned to the rotund geographer and said, "We need now but follow the plan expressed by 'Old Tut' in his notebook, and, unless unforseen events have overtaken the *Chester Alan Arthur,* we shall quickly discover the whereabouts of that craft and learn of the doubtlessly intriguing exploits of her crew."

"Indeed," said Mr. Blount, beside himself with elation at the success to this point of the joint endeavor of Miss Taphammer and himself, "I shall rejoice to greet

once again our colleague Thintwhistle, and assure myself to his safety and well-being. Although I do worry
somewhat over the reception which we shall receive
upon our return home.

"Removing such building materials as we did for
Mayor von der Lucan's feed and harness shop, and
from Sheriff Callister's dry goods emporium, will hardly rest well with those persons. And then there is the
matter of our own truancy from our respective pedagogical duties."

Miss Taphammer said, "Mr. Blount, did we not
leave behind *billets-doux* explaining the extreme ur-
gency our requirements, listing all items we had removed, and pledging to make good immediately upon
our return from our journey?" Without waiting for the
geographer's assent, she went on, "And as for our absenting ourselves from our classes, why piano strings
and piccolos, if those children miss us I shall be very
surprised indeed. Certainly the lives of three missing
persons are of greater importance to the town of Buffalo Falls then are a few days of discordant wheezes by
a Normal School orchestra or the fact that a roomful of
adolescents memorizing the capitals of the Latin American republics will have to do so without your super-
vision."

"Mmm, mmm, mmm," said Mr. Blount. "Well, I suppose it's too late to change anything now, Miss Taphammer. If you are so convinced of the rightness of
our actions, I suppose we had as well proceed."

"Thank you, Winchester," said Miss Taphammer,
sliding the *Susan B. Anthony* into a steeper course of
ascent, so that before very long she had raised her
nose above the clouds themselves, and continued to
rise into a darkening sky, there above the rolling hills
and prosperous farmsteads of the Middle West.

"This is a most interesting section of the Republic," Mr. Blount commented, "comprising some twenty-two states with an aggregate population of nearly forty millions, with a combined agricultural and industrial production in excess of twelve billions of dollars per year, and producing most of the beef cattle, pork, wheat, corn, and barley consumed in the United States."

"Thank you," said Miss Taphammer.

"Oh, that is the merest sample of the knowledge which I possess concerning this interesting region. I can continue indefinitely if you are really interested."

"I am really fascinated," replied Miss Taphammer, "but I fear that the operation of the ether-flyer does not permit me to offer you the full attention your lecture clearly deserves. Do you think you could hold back the remainder, my dear friend, until an occasion upon which I may attend you undistracted?"

"Ah, of course! I am so pleased that your interest is of so high a degree. You know, Miss Taphammer, there are many persons uninterested in the fascinating subject of geography!"

"The poorer for it, I am sure," said Miss Taphammer.

The exterior windows of the *Susan B. Anthony* now showed a starry blackness rather than the familiar blue sky of western Pennsylvania, for behind the improved ether-flyer the lush earth had receded to become a mere ball suspended in the heavens, mottled with whites and blues, greens and browns, rotating in slow splendor upon its well-fixed but invisible axis.

Ahead lay the white disk of Diana, the ruler of the night skies and the destination of the *Susan B. Anthony* and her sparse crew.

And in whatever strange place in the etheric sea which was occupied by the original ether-flyer, the former *Chester A. Arthur* now redubbed *Crispus Attucks* moved through space along a predetermined path, her paddle wheels revolving in the etheric current. In her rear compartment her somewhat tipsy commanding officer, Menelik XX Chaka, was startled to hear from the direction of the galleon *Escarabajo de Plata* the unmistakable loud report of a cannon being discharged.

Chaka whirled from the furnace over which he had been watching and raced to a porthole. There before his eyes the Spanish craft could be seen heeling over upon her hull, her masts and spars turned all topsy-turvy as the ship capsized. There was a sound of another cannon, and the *Escarabajo* added a new element of motion to her strange behavior, then a series of shots and the galleon entered a strange and alarming mode of behavior, whirling more and more rapidly through a series of maneuvers so complex that Chaka found his primitive but cunning mind unable to fathom their pattern.

Suddenly the *Escarabajo* emitted a glow of coloration so weird that Chaka could identify none of the tints, at the end of which display the lights disappeared from the sky, and with them the galleon itself.

Chaka turned uncuriously from the window and returned to the first matter of business at hand, the furnace. Already Chaka had heard the satisfying *clunk!* of the pursuing ship containing the miniature Professor Thintwhistle and Herkimer, and watched with gleeful satisfaction through the iron door-grating of the furnace the flames leaping and roaring about the tiny craft.

Now he returned to the furnace, cackling with a

drunken glee at the approach of his moment of final triumph over "Old Tut" and "Herk." Donning asbestos gloves and smoked-lensed goggles he flung open the furnace door and peered within. Instead of roaring flames the interior of the furnace was coated with a thick layer of white frost, in the midst of which stood the strange little ship.

Through the windows of the ship Chaka saw the tiny fingers of Professor Thintwhistle pointing at him, scurrying about, moving the controls. Dumbfounded, Chaka stood unmoving as the small propulsion devices mounted between the ridges of the strange ship swivelled to point at him. The ship rose from the floor of the furnace and began to move toward him; simultaneously the self-appointed captain of the *Attucks* felt a strange coldness seize him.

Briefly the cold became painfully intense, then the combination of the purloined sherry which he had downed, the shock of seeing the Professor alive and his ship intact in the furnace, and the terrible blast of cold which he had received, rendered Menelik XX Chaka, commander of the ether-flyer *Crispus Attucks*, unconscious.

In the royal seat of the Lunite Commonwealth, matters were moving from bad to worse. The Palace of Peace and Joy had been filled to overflowing with merrymakers, entertainers, servitors and celebrants of every sort in hopes of restoring the well-being and favorable disposition of Selena the Queen of the Moon. That noble lady had striven with all of her inconsiderable will and might to accomplish such recovery unaided, but had failed to do so, hence, acting upon the advice of Lady Melanopla, she ordered a giant festival to fill every room and corner of the Palace.

In the main chamber of the royal apartment lush cushions lay scattered about the marble floor, where royal ladies and their courtiers sprawled at their leisure, sipping at mellow wines of gold and ruby, or accepting moist fruits of every description. The lighting of the chamber was low and everchanging, as torches of special chemical compositions flared crimson and azure, emerald and gold, pink, yellow, lavender and vermilion.

The tinkling of crystal instruments, an orchestra whose sounds were so delicate and subtle as to penetrate the entire ambiance of the room, lent a rhythm and melody that pervaded the entire scene, while in the pit in the center of the room, the great ladies of the court were amused by the gyrations of specially trained dancing boys whose curriculum from earliest childhood had been directed solely toward the goal of providing such titillation as might be required by the powerful and the wealthy.

Still Selena felt unwell. She pushed aside sweetmeats, threw her crystal goblet upon the floor with such violence that shattered bits flew to all parts of the room, and ordered the entertainment to cease. In but moments the chamber was vacant save for Selena, her most trusted ladies in waiting, and the chief court physician, Dr. Ruvuma.

"Never has the ruler of the Lunites been so unfortunate as am I," wailed Selena. "My ears ring, my head swims, my stomach rises and falls within my body as though it were a ship on stormy oceans!

"Woe, oh woe to the Lunites, and woe to Selena their Queen!"

"Now, now, Your Majesty," said Dr. Ruvuma soothingly, "you ought not to despair. We will find a cure yet."

"Do your best, Ruvuma," the Queen replied, "but I despair indeed of being cured. I fear that my death is inevitable, leaving the throne of the Lunites vacant and leading to a war of succession that will destroy the weal of my beloved people."

"It seems clear to me," Dr. Ruvuma replied, "that some disruptive element must have introduced itself into Your Royal Majesty's body at the time of your recent wound. Were you but purged, it might be that that foreign influence might be removed."

"Anything, anything, Ruvuma. Give me your purgative and let us on with it," moaned the Queen.

CHAPTER 17
The Octahedral Globe

Quetzalcoatl, the great feathered serpent, wove its wary way through the inner darkness, its many-faceted eyes peering this way and that as the serpent's movements caused them to be directed toward one feature or another of the endless and trackless void. Within the head of the weaving serpent lights shone, lights which created, from the exterior of the serpent, the illusion of a powerful and sinister life, gleaming forth from the brilliant eyes.

Mictlantecutli, steersman of the serpent, turned momentarily from his efforts at the sound of the voice of Xochipilli, carried to him from the observer's station located at the dorsal end of the serpent. "My commander," Xochipilli intoned, "but peer from the right eye of the god and observe a portent placed in the heavens for us to see."

His golden ornaments jangling, Mictlantecutli turned to do as Xochipilli had asked. In a moment he rose from his couch and stood gazing at the weird sight before his eyes: a strange object in the void, great discs seemingly affixed to its flanks, revolving at terrible speed, horns or fangs upraised above its crown, spewing forth tongues of flame, bright sparks and black cloudlets of smoke.

"A xiucoatl?" mused Mictlantecutli.

Before Xochipilli had made reply, the flame and smoke ceased to emerge from the strange object, the discs slowed their movement and were seen to be great revolving wheels.

"A xiucoatl perhaps, my commander," Xochipilli said. "A sacred creature if it is, if not a god."

Mictlantecutli mused for moments, gazing at the strange sight. If it was indeed a xiucoatl, or fire serpent, then the Book of Destiny, the tonamatl, would dictate a proper course of action. Mictlantecutli laid on his most splendid ornaments, anointed himself with holy oil, and consulted the tonamatl.

As he did so a great glowing light arose in the sky beyond the xiucoatl, brightened, faded, then disappeared. Mictlantecutli turned from the Book to the tiller of the feathered serpent and directed its weaving, graceful course toward the seemingly quiescent fire serpent. Very shortly the two creatures would be joined and the steersman would direct Xochipilli, his observer, to reconnoitre the condition of the fire serpent and report back to him.

The *Quetzalcoatl*, feathers waving as it seemed more to swim than to fly through the universal ether, made its approach to the strange xiucoatl. At length the two were side-by-side. Mictlantecutli performed the needful acts to cause the *Quetzalcoatl* to wrap its feathered length about the shorter body of the xiucoatl.

A transit was arranged between the octahedral globe in which the observer Xochipilli performed his duties, and the portal of the strange xiucoatl. Xochipilli made his formal leave-taking of Mictlantecutli and the feathered serpent, and made his way into the strange xiucoatl.

Earlier, within the furnace of the *Crispus Attucks*,

Professor Thintwhistle and Herkimer had felt their Felisian coldopter, the *Frigidia*, being drawn irresistibly into the terrible flames by Menelik XX Chaka's insidious magnetic device. As the *Frigidia* was surrounded by the searing fire, Professor Thintwhistle's far-famed mind acted rapidly. Only seconds remained before the flames would heat the *Frigidia* to an unbearable level of temperature; the Professor, his aide Herkimer and their tiny mascot Cleopatra would quickly expire, shortly following which the entire coldopter would be reduced to a smoldering pile of ashes and slag, while the fiendishly traitorous Jefferson Jackson Clay escaped scot-free!

Moving with incredible swiftness for a gentleman of his advancing years, the Professor adjusted the *Frigidia*'s power plants to their maximum level of power. Instantly the Felisian machines began to draw heat from the flames directly ahead of them. In the merest instant of time the flames were reduced to mere flickers, then these too disappeared.

Professor Thintwhistle spun the helm of the *Frigidia*, turning the cold-field generators this way and that, instantly dousing the flames at which they were pointed, until, less than a minute after the arrival of the coldopter within its furnace, the *Crispus Attucks* was without power, its furnace entirely doused and its interior covered with a layer of frost and ice!

The Professor remained at the controls of the *Frigidia*, Herkimer loyally at his elbow. In a moment the door of the furnace was opened. A giant grinning face surmounted by an askew commodore's hat leered down into the furnace. As the eyes widened in wonder and realization the face's expression altered to one of shock and alarm.

Professor Thintwhistle adjusted the helm of the coldopter, shoved the power control forward once again, and watched for the effect yet to come. Jefferson Jackson Clay, or Menelik XX Chaka—for it was indeed the unworthy servant whose features had filled the door of the furnace—seemed to grow frozen into immobility as he stood facing the coldopter.

In a moment the Felisian ship rose from its place in the furnace, floated forward through the opening, carefully circled the immobile servant, and floated downward to land upon the floor of the ether-flyer. "Ho, lad!" boomed Professor Thintwhistle in his loudest and gayest voice, "did you think we would ever again lay eyes on the inside of the *Chester Alan Arthur?*"

"Not I," admitted Herkimer, adjusting his straw skimmer upon his head and bending to straighten the elastic bottoms of his knickerbocker trousers. "But I suppose that now all is well, dear Professor. Is it not?"

"Nearly so, dear boy, nearly so, save for a few minor details. For the moment let us debark from this borrowed craft and see to the binding of our prisoner, for it is as such that we must presently regard the blackamoor." So saying, and shaking his head sadly so that his graying locks and beard swung about his head like waves of the great gray ocean, the Professor proceeded to exit from the coldopter, followed closely by Herkimer.

The two walked once about the interior of the ether-flyer, savoring at once their joy at being, at last, somehow "at home" once again, while simultaneously marveling at the fixtures and appurtenances of the ether-flyer as seen from the apparent viewpoint of a creature the size of a housecat. As the two searched for materials with which to bind the temporarily immobilized house man, there was a sudden thump and, looking upward, they observed the portholes of the *Arthur* to be covered with what seemed to be feathers!

"What can this mean, O mentor?" Herkimer pleaded piteously of his more elderly companion.

Before the pedagogue could reply, the door from the *Arthur*'s saloon to her rear quarters swung open and a person of strange mien and green garb, wearing a feathered cap, stepped through. Turning his eyes from one side to the other he espied first the frozen form of Jefferson, then the tiny figures of the Professor and Herkimer.

The Professor was the first to speak, calling out to the newcomer, "Ho there, young fellow! Who are you and what are you doing aboard our ether-flyer?" But the strange person ignored this and all further imprecations from the two tiny figures. Instead he hastily crossed the compartment, seized the house man by the wrists and began chafing them.

Quickly the mobility of the erstwhile servant returned, whereupon he and the stranger in green bent to confront the Professor and Herkimer. Filled with righteous outrage at this conduct, Professor Thint-whistle launched upon a justified tirade against Jefferson, only to be seized from behind, along with Herkimer, and raised into the air by the green-clad stranger!

Raging impotently he saw Jefferson disappear in the direction of the pantry, to return bearing a large glass jar into which the stranger unceremoniously dumped both himself and Herkimer. Before the two could do more than begin to protest this outrage, a perforated lid was screwed onto the jar, the jar held securely by Jefferson, and the stranger, bowing ceremoniously, turned and left the ether-flyer, having uttered not a single word!

Shortly, with a sibilant, slithering sound, the feathers disappeared from the windows of the ether-flyer and Chaka, his tipsiness gone with the strange experiences he had undergone, walked with the jar in his hands to the Captain's Vernada, where he deposited the container on the chart board beside the ether-flyer's control panel.

The Professor and Herkimer were clearly visible inside their glass prison beating tiny fists upon its walls and screaming imprecations at their captor. Chaka surveyed their plight for a while, then, assuming for the moment the lackadaisical expression and slovenly manner of speech so long associated with the ignorant Jefferson Jackson Clay, he brought his great, lugubrious eyes down to a position near those of the Professor and Herkimer, and said, "Yowsah, boss. What y'all want me to do now?"

"You rascal!" screamed the Professor. "You blackguard! Turncoat! Unworthy creature! First let us out of this ridiculous prison! Then we will tell you where to steer the *Arthur,* so that we may return our borrowed coldopter and regain the phlogiston which will restore us to our proper stature!"

"And be quick about it, Jefferson, or you shall rue your misdeeds even more than you otherwise should!" Herkimer added, his skimmer bobbing with his rage and excitation.

"Ah's sorry, bosses," the blackamoor replied, still feigning the sloppy habits of speech he had so long affected. "But ah cain't do that. Fust of all, ain't no mo' *Arthur* nohow. Dis yere ether-flyer now de *Crispus Attucks.* Secon', ain't no mo' Jefferson neithah. Ah's none other than Menelik XX Chaka, Captain of the *Attucks.*"

With these last words he assumed the upright bearing and confident tone which had been demonstrated since his absenting himself from the environs of the planet Felisia aleph in his stolen ether-flyer. "I have liberated this craft, little men," Chaka intoned, "and as for returning to Felisia, that is another question altogether, one which will require serious contemplation on the part of the captain of the *Attucks,* that is, myself.

"It was just a lucky break," he went on musingly, "that my comrades aboard the feathered serpent received my message when we first encountered one another, and stayed near enough at hand to provide help when it was needed. Your little trick with the freezing devices nearly worked, but then counterrevolutions are never successful in the long run."

So saying, Menelik XX Chaka strode majestically away from the common glass jar containing the Professor and Herk, and halted, to stand gazing through the *Crispus Attucks'* forward port.

Before his astounded eyes the heavens were reeling; stars danced and gyrated in their places, clouds of cosmic dust swirled and flowed, great clusters of bright matter seemed to invert themselves, huge flashes of colors darted here and there, while the very blackness of space itself writhed and wrenched about. The *Crispus Attucks* jerked and shuddered beneath his feet, her now powerless paddle wheels whirring madly as cosmic winds of hurricane proportion passed over them, while the now anachronistic portrait bust of President Arthur spun wildly as etheric winds twirled the carven wooden propeller.

Menelik XX Chaka clutched at the control panel of the ether-flyer, barely able to retain his feet as the very fabric of the intra-Selenate cosmos twisted, spun and shook. Still, with one hand he kept hold of the bottle containing his two small prisoners, never letting it be dashed from its place on the chart table, lest its occupants either be injured or make their escape.

At last the *Attucks* and the heavens about her grew still and silent, but it seemed to be the stillness and silence that anticipates a coming climax of consummate violence rather than that which heralds an enduring period of calm.

While in the Palace of Peace and Joy, Queen Selena writhed and sweated, thrashing about the main chamber of the royal apartment. Her personal physician, Dr. Ruvuma, held the hand of his monarch, mopped her perspiring brow from time to time, and murmured encouraging words. After a time the monarch settled into a position of greater repose. She turned her brilliant eyes upon the court physician and said "Ruvuma, the purgative has failed."

"*Au contraire*, Your Majesty," Ruvuma responded, "it has followed its course exactly as I expected. You are experiencing a mere momentary respite. Perhaps a breath of fresh air would aid Your Majesty before the crisis which is yet to come. I believe that our treatment is about to prove itself highly successful!"

So saying the physician flung open a marble-framed window. His monarch crossed the room and leaned her elbows upon the window sill, eagerly drinking in the thin but refreshing lunar atmosphere.

High above the capital city of the Lunites, there moved at this very moment the improved ether-flyer *Susan B. Anthony*. Her captain and pilot was the capable Miss Olivia Taphammer. The remainder of her crew was comprised entirely of Mr. Winchester Blount, the pink and rotund geography instructor, who at this very moment was exclaiming over the sights which he beheld beneath the little ship.

"Oh, marvelous!" Mr. Blount cried. "Oh, how wonderful! Miss Taphammer, conceive of it, an entire world to map and explore! What wonders shall we behold, what strange creatures and weird selenographical features shall we observe! Oh, ecstasy, how they shall marvel back at the Faculty Club, or better yet, the Buffalo Falls Scientific Society!"

He turned from the window for a moment to face his companion, whose concentration upon the course ahead and the instruments in her hands had never wavered. "You will consent to co-author a paper with me, will you not, Miss Taphammer? Just imagine it, *A Journey to the Moon and the Investigation Thereof*, by O. Taphammer and W. Blount!"

"An amusing prospect, Mr. Blount," said Miss Taphammer, not taking her eyes from the window before her, "but you forget that our journey is not in the least unprecedented, that Professor Thintwhistle and his two companions have already ventured into this region, and that it is our paramount duty to locate them, and offer aid if it is needful."

"Of course, of course," mumbled the geographer, his pink hands fluttering before him. "Still, we may not be entirely without glory upon our return. Is not Stanley as well known as Livingstone?"

Before she could make reply, Miss Taphammer was astounded to see beneath the *Susan B. Anthony* the incredible shape of the Lunite capital, its gardens and canals, dwellings and shops and manufactories converging upon the drill field of the Ice Cream Brigade and the Royal Palace of Peace and Joy.

"Behold, Winchester," gasped Miss Taphammer, "a city! There shall we initiate our inquiry as to the whereabouts of the Professor and his companions!" So saying she altered the settings of the controls of the

Susan B. Anthony, which sturdy craft began steadily to lower itself toward the Palace itself.

Within the Palace, in the main chamber of the royal apartment, Queen Selena found that the cool and fragrant air she inhaled at her window lent but a moment of pleasure before her form was wracked by a single, climactic convulsion. The alert Dr. Ruvuma was at her side, ready to place a comforting hand upon the bare royal back.

Selena pursed her royal lips, puffed her royal cheeks, her countenance darkened with concentration and the rush of the royal blood, and with a loud *poof!* a small object flew from her mouth, circled lazily once before her, and landed softly in her hand.

The Queen turned to show the strange object to Dr. Ruvuma. As she did so an opening appeared in its side and a black man hardly bigger than the nail upon her royal pinky stepped out. The eyes of the monarch and her physician popped wide in astonishment. The Queen said, "There it is, O wise Ruvuma. You have cured me and won anew our royal favor upon your house and yourself. But what is it?"

Upon the palm of her majesty's hand the black man stood, facing up, and in a voice barely audible to the two Lunites cried out "Greetings! In the name of the revolutionary independent freebooter *Crispus Attucks,* I, Captain Menelik XX Chaka, offer this gift!" He held forth a tiny bottle in which the Queen and her physician were able barely to make out two figures of unbelievable smallness cavorting angrily.

"A wonder, clearly a wonder! Welcome, tiny man, to our court. Your gift shall reside in the Lunite Museum and you shall be an honored guest at our court for as long as you wish to remain."

The recovered Queen gently carried Chaka, the jar,

and the ether-flyer to a splendid cushion, where she placed them with great care and gentleness. Already word had gone out from the royal apartment of the cure of the Queen, and all of the nation of the Lunites celebrated the happy recovery.

In their tiny jar Professor Thintwhistle and Herkimer raged and gesticulated impotently.

On the splendid cushion Menelik XX Chaka reclined comfortably, carrying on revolutionary discourse with a steady stream of admiring citizens of the moon. Already Queen Selena had been convinced of the justice of abolishing her hereditary throne and declaring her nation a republic.

In the sky above the Palace, still no larger than a pretty speck but growing larger by the moment, the improved ether-flyer *Susan B. Anthony* settled toward the lunar surface.

And at this juncture we take our leave of Professor Thintwhistle, Herkimer, Miss Taphammer, Mr. Blount, Selena, Cleopatra the cat mother, and all of the others with whom we have adventured of late. If you would like to delve further into their destinies, reader, let us make a bargain.

If you will promise to be very good at all times, to obey every rule set forth in the Book of Destiny, and most particularly to give justice to all those who have been denied it, then I will record for you the further adventures of Professor Thintwhistle and his Incredible Ether-Flyer.

In the meanwhile, think well and act rightly, for who among us all ever knows when he may find himself in a jar?

26 Weeks on *The New York Times* Bestseller List!
"Terrifying, suspenseful, mind shattering."
Washington Post

DELIVERANCE

by James Dickey

This novel, by one of America's finest poets, is a tale of violent adventure and inner discovery. Four men embark on a canoe trip down a wild section of a river in the heartland of today's South. When two of the group are attacked viciously and perversely by mountaineers, a mildly adventurous canoe trip explodes into a gruesome nightmare of horror and murder.

"The limit of dramatic tension ... a novel that will curl your toes!"   *The New York Times*

Now a major motion picture from
Warner Brothers starring Burt Reynolds and
Jon Voight

A DELL BOOK $1.25

"One of the 10 most notable novels of the decade."
—*Time* magazine

CATCH-22

by JOSEPH HELLER

Catch-22 is a comic novel about World War II. Set on the tiny island of Pianosa in the Mediterranean Sea, the novel is devoted to a series of impossible, illogical adventures engaged in by members of the 256th bombing squadron, an unlikely combat group whose fanatical commander, Colonel Cathcart, keeps increasing the men's quota of missions. The book's central character is Captain Yossarian, the squadron's lead bombardier. Eventually, after Cathcart has exterminated nearly all of Yossarian's buddies through suicidal missions, Yossarian decides to desert. "The best American novel to come out of World War II . . . the best American novel that has come out of anywhere in years."
—Nelson Algren, *The Nation*

Don't miss the superb
Mike Nichols film from Paramount.

A DELL BOOK $1.50

If you cannot obtain copies of this title from your local bookseller, just send the price (plus 25c per copy for handling and postage) to Dell Books, Post Office Box 1000, Pinebrook, N. J. 07058.

KURT VONNEGUT, JR.

"One of the best living American writers."

—Graham Greene

CAT'S CRADLE

A fantasy about the end of the world—replete with atomic scientists, ugly Americans, gorgeous Sex Queens, Caribbean dictators and God.

A Dell Book: $1.25
Also available as a Delta paperback: $1.95

GOD BLESS YOU, MR. ROSEWATER

A satirical and black-humored novel about Eliot Rosewater, president of the Rosewater Foundation, dedicated to bring love into the hearts of everyone.

A Dell Book: $1.25
Also available as a Delta paperback: $1.95

THE SIRENS OF TITAN

At the same time a deep and comic reflection on the human dilemma, this novel follows the richest man in America, Malachi Constant, as he gives up a life of unequaled indulgence to pursue the irresistible Sirens of Titan.

A Dell Book: $1.25
Also available as a Delta paperback: $2.25

SLAUGHTERHOUSE-5, or The Children's Crusade

A supremely unconventional war novel based on the experiences of the author as a prisoner of war during the catastrophic fire-bombing of Dresden during World War II. The hero of his story also survives the fire-bombing and is to some extent reconciled to life as it is lived on Earth. But Vonnegut is not, and in this remarkable book he has expressed his terrible outrage.

A Dell Book: 95c
Also available as a Delta paperback: $1.95

WELCOME TO THE MONKEY HOUSE

The long-awaited volume which brings together the finest of Kurt Vonnegut, Jr.'s shorter works. It is a funny, sad, explosive, wildly gyrating gathering, a mind-boggling grab bag in which every selection is a winner.

A Dell Book: $1.25
Also available as a Delta paperback: $1.95

If you cannot obtain copies of these titles from your local bookseller, just send the price (plus 25c per copy for handling and postage) to Dell Books, Post Office Box 1000, Pinebrook, N. J. 07058.

HOW MANY OF THESE DELL BESTSELLERS HAVE YOU READ?

1. **THE MAN WHO LOVED CAT DANCING**
   by Marilyn Durham $1.75

2. **LAST TANGO IN PARIS** by Robert Alley $1.75

3. **THE BRAND-NAME CARBOHYDRATE GRAM**
   COUNTER by Corinne T. Netzer $1.50

4. **THE EROTIC LIFE OF THE AMERICAN WIFE**
   by Natalie Gittelson $1.75

5. **GEORGE S. KAUFMAN** by Howard Teichmann $1.95

6. **THE TRUTH ABOUT WEIGHT CONTROL**
   by Dr. Neil Solomon $1.50

7. **MEAT ON THE HOOF** by Gary Shaw $1.50

8. **MAFIA, USA** by Nicholas Gage $1.75

9. **THE HAPPY HOOKER** by Xaviera Hollander $1.50

10. **THE WATER IS WIDE** by Pat Conroy $1.50

11. **THE OSTERMAN WEEKEND** by Robert Ludlum $1.50

12. **11 HARROWHOUSE** by Gerald A. Browne $1.50

13. **DISRAELI IN LOVE** by Maurice Edelman $1.50

14. **WILL THERE REALLY BE A MORNING?**
    by Frances Farmer $1.50

15. **A PSYCHIATRIST'S HEAD**
    by Martin Shepard, M.D. $1.50

16. **DEEP THROAT** by D. M. Perkins $1.50

If you cannot obtain copies of these titles from your local bookseller, just send the price (plus 25c per copy for handling and postage) to Dell Books, Post Office Box 1000, Pinebrook, N. J. 07058.